Greyla

GIN AND M

Josephine Mary Wedderburn Pullein-Thompson was born in April 1924, the second of four children of a school-master badly wounded in the First World War and the novelist Joanna Cannan. Like many women before her, Miss Cannan had turned to writing to support her family; as well as writing detective stories and literary novels, she single-handedly created the 'pony book', a new genre which inspired her three daughters, Josephine, Christine and Diana, to emulate and make their own. All three sisters were expert horsewomen and ran their own Grove Riding School near Henley-on-Thames. When Josephine's early ambition to become a vet was thwarted by an unconventional and rather haphazard education, she turned to writing with her first books being published in 1946. Over the next 50 years she wrote over thirty more pony books, a handful of non-fiction equestrian titles, and three novels for adults; the murder mysteries *Gin and Murder* (1959), *They Died in the Spring* (1960) and *Murder Strikes Pink* (1963). She had long involvement with the British branch of International PEN, which campaigns for writers' freedom in authoritarian regimes, and was awarded the MBE in 1984 for services to literature. Josephine Pullein-Thompson died in June 2014, aged 90.

GIN AND MURDER

JOSEPHINE PULLEIN-THOMPSON

Greyladies

Published by
Greyladies
an imprint of The Old Children's Bookshelf

© Josephine Pullein-Thompson 1959
Design and layout © Shirley Neilson 2014
Cover image courtesy of & © Mary Evans Picture Library

ISBN   978-1-907503-37-5

Set in Sylfaen / Perpetua
Printed and bound by CPI Group (UK) Ltd., Croydon CR0 4YY

CHAPTER ONE

THE MOMENT she reached the Chadwicks' it became apparent that Clara Broughton was in an advanced state of intoxication. Mark, her husband, who had found her quiet and gloomy and judged her comparatively sober at home, cursed himself for having brought her.

As they left their coats in the tiny dining-room of the cottage he lectured her. 'You're not to have more than one drink, Clara. If you do you'll pass out; you're half seas over already. Do you hear, Clara? Only one drink.' He spoke to her as though she were a small, naughty child or a dear and disobedient dog.

'All right, Mark,' she answered huskily. 'Just one little drink. Dear Mark.' She clutched his arm affectionately and then exclaimed in tones of anguish, 'God, I need that drink.'

It was hopeless, Mark thought wearily, but if she did pass out it wouldn't be the first time. People must know what to expect by now and, if they didn't like it they needn't ask them—a good many of them didn't, he reminded himself bitterly.

'Come on, Mark, shtop dithering,' commanded Clara, 'You're going to see your golden girl.'

Mark sighed. All right, he thought, I do want to see Hilary, though what good it'll do me, God knows; and he followed his wife down the passage to the long, beamed drawing-room. As usual he forgot the lowness of the doorway and cracked his head on an oak beam. 'Hell!' he

1

said loudly and then added, 'Sorry, Elizabeth,' as, rubbing his head ruefully, he gazed down at his hostess.

'If you never said anything worse than that, Mark, we'd have no cause to complain,' said Elizabeth Chadwick. Charlie Chadwick, who had already provided Clara with a drink, asked, 'Whisky, Mark?'

'Please. I can't risk naval concoctions on Friday nights.'

Chadwick handed Mark his drink. 'Will you draw the Lindens first, tomorrow?'

'Yes, if the wind stays where it is. And then Scrubs Wood, but don't let on or we'll have all those idle bastards unboxing their horses at the Lindens. Then if there is a fox lying there it'll be in East Wintshire before hounds get to the draw. That's the worst of these small covers.'

'Mum's the word,' promised Chadwick, and with a decanter of sherry in one hand and a cocktail shaker in the other, he began a tour of the room, replenishing the glasses of his guests.

Mark Broughton looked round for his host's daughter and, when his eyes found her the usual mixture of pain and joy assailed him. She was looking lovely. Mark never saw what women wore or how their hair was done; it was the whole which pleased or failed to please him. He liked them to delight his eye as did a well-proportioned blood horse or a view of unspoiled country. But now he noticed that she was talking in an animated way to that bloody man Vickers. Mark scowled furiously across the room and swallowed the rest of his whisky in an angry gulp. Damn the fellow. Why had Charlie asked him here? Now he needed another drink.

Clara Broughton was enjoying herself. The room was behaving rather like a ship in a storm, but they always did nowadays; one got used to it, women were so much more adaptable than men. What fun, she thought, a party; a room full of lovely people. 'Don't you agree, Steve?' she asked, as a face she knew emerged from the mist.

'Do I agree with what, Mrs. Broughton?' asked Stephen Denton.

'That women are more adaptable than men? Oh, Steve, it's *nice* to see you,' she went on without giving him time to reply. 'You're looking terribly handsome, such lovely long legs—I always have liked men with long legs. Does your pretty little wife still love you? I'm sure she must.'

'Well I hope so, though I did hear some muttering the other day about married life being spent at the sink. The poor girl's got to put up with another fifty years of me yet; my family have always been octogenarians. It's a sobering thought.' He spoke lightly, but it was compassion which he felt as he looked down at Clara. You poor silly woman, he thought, you look a worse wreck every time I see you. He observed the ragbag confusion of unmatching and unfashionable garments, the mask of make-up slapped heavily and lopsidedly upon the disintegrating face, the tangle of pepper-and-salt hair. You're only about ten years older than I am, he thought, it's not very pleasant to think what alcohol must have done to your inside. 'Here *is* Sonia,' he said aloud. 'Darling, Mrs. Broughton hopes you still appreciate me after eleven months of married life.'

They stood close together; Stephen tall, lean and fair with blue eyes and a humorous mouth in a good-natured face and Sonia small, pretty and kittenish, a woman who realized that her face and her figure were her fortune and made them her life's work.

She said: 'He's not as good as he looks, Mrs. Broughton. And it's no joke being married to a vet—meals at all hours and Steve out half the night—but still, I wouldn't change him.'

Despite her animated conversation with Guy Vickers, Hilary Chadwick had seen Mark the moment he entered the room. In fact she had made several attempts to move in his direction but had each time been skilfully forestalled by her companion. Now she had stopped listening to Guy, whose conversation was amusing if rather dependent on personalities, and was considering her desire for escape. Guy was good-looking, rich, horsey, unmarried and thirty-four. If she married Guy she would have marvellous clothes and lovely horses, she would have a fashionable wedding and her parents would be pleased. The human heart, thought Hilary, being the contrary organ it is, refuses to leap to order at the sight of such things. Mine won't leap for Guy, but when it persists in leaping at the sight of the wholly unattainable can one continue to consider its views?

'Guy,' she said, 'I've thought of an excuse for the Sellocks—that is, if you still want to take me out tomorrow night.'

'You'll dine with me? *Wunderbar!*' he said, and he looked so pleased her heart was touched.

'I shall be a very tedious companion,' she told him. 'I'm always half asleep after hunting.'

4

Noticing Mark Broughton standing alone by the door, Colonel Holmes-Waterford crossed the room to speak to him. Both men were dark, of equal height and the same age but there their similarity ended. Douglas Holmes-Waterford was of lighter build and wore his well-made clothes with an unobtrusive air; but it was his pallor, his quiet voice and his self command that made him seem the antithesis of Broughton, who managed to look tanned even in January, and whose smile and scowl came and went with his turbulent temper.

'Mark,' said Holmes-Waterford, 'stop looking like the spectre at the feast. What's eating you, as they say?'

'That bloody man Vickers,' answered Mark promptly. 'I can't think why Charlie has to ask him here. He knows he's been ratting round after a joint mastership because I told him so myself.'

'My dear fellow,' Douglas Holmes-Waterford was choosing his words with care, 'it's perfectly obvious Vickers, who will one day be a millionaire—or as near as no matter—is a catch for any girl. In the circumstances you really can't blame Charlie for putting his daughter's prospects before your quarrel.'

'Hell and damn the circumstances! I'd like to wring Vickers' neck.'

'Oh come, he 's not such a bad lad; he rides well and they say that he's practically a certainty for the next Olympics. I'm sure the whole thing's been grossly exaggerated by Clinkerton. For a start I can't help feeling that a man like Vickers would fly a bit higher than the West Wintshire if he wanted to take a pack of hounds.'

5

'We'll let him fly higher then. Let him take his infernal money to the shires and stop there.'

'Oh really, Mark.' Holmes-Waterford's voice was disapproving. I think I'd better go and have a word with him before the whole situation gets out of control. I'll find out if there is anything behind this conversation with Clinkerton. But you know, as well as I do, that our secretary's a bit of an old rumourmonger. Probably there's nothing much to it. I've no doubt it was, at the most, a tentative suggestion, and also no doubt that the committee's only consideration was the chance of saving you expense.'

'When I want a joint master I'll tell them,' said Mark Broughton. 'And if they don't like the way I run the hunt let them get up and say so at the proper time and place.'

Only one drink, Clara Broughton thought. Be a good girl, Clara. Poor Mark, he can't get his golden girl. Go and cut her out, Clara, go and talk to Guy what's his name. Give poor Mark his chance. There's a mountain and God knows how many woods between you, but it's not his fault. Don't cry, Clara, she told herself as she weaved uncertainly across the room, remember you're at a party.

Captain Bewley was making the most of the occasion. Free drinks did not come his way every day and Charlie certainly knew how to knock up cocktails. Pleasantly exhilarated, his cigarette case filled surreptitiously from the box on the pembroke table, all he wanted now was a nice, friendly girl. But, he thought, there was no fun to be had here. Hilary was far too high-minded, Antonia Brockenhurst was the most undersexed female in the county, and that pretty little cat Sonia Denton was still jealously guarded by Steve. There was only Clara. He'd go and talk to Clara, he decided. Dipso she might be, but she was still worth two of all the rest. Vickers was looking at her disdainfully, but he only saw a sodden wreck; he hadn't known her five years ago. She'd never been a pretty little bit like Sonia; too much character for that, but God, she'd been attractive and good fun. There'd been no one to touch Clara in Wintshire.

'Birds of a feather, Clara, birds of a feather,' he said, breaking in on the confused conversation she was having with Vickers.

'Oh, Bob darling, how lovely. Dear Bob, such fun. You're so wicked; you always bring out the worst in me.'

'Come and sit in a corner,' said Bewley. 'A dark corner, and we'll get drunk.'

Sonia Denton was careful to keep a group of people between her and Guy Vickers. She hoped he would have the sense to keep away from her; but you couldn't trust Guy, a few drinks and he threw discretion to the winds. She didn't want another ugly scene; it had been a terrible shock to discover that good-natured, easygoing Steve could behave like that, could say such dreadful things. She loved Steve, but one couldn't help wondering what life would have been like if one had met Guy first. It was like hats, thought Sonia, as soon as you bought one you had to avoid looking in shop windows in case you saw another you liked better. Once you were married you ought to avoid parties, they were only shop windows for human relationships. How clearly I think, I'm quite intelligent really, she decided. People don't realize it, they think that I'm just decorative, but there's no need to look a mess because you've got brains.

Elizabeth Chadwick, who, with her beautiful complexion, curling grey hair and enormous brown eyes, did not look old enough to have a daughter of twenty-seven, was listening with half an ear to Antonia Brockenhurst and wondering why they had asked her. Thank goodness Hilary's not as horsey as this, she thought, as Wednesday's run was retold fence by fence. She looked for her daughter across the room and saw her talking to Mark. Thank God Hilary's sensible, she thought, trying to stifle her misgivings as she saw the expression on Mark's face . . . Guy was a nice boy, a little spoiled, perhaps, but you can't have everything in life. If Hilary married him she wouldn't have this losing battle against poverty, wouldn't have to divide her time between the sink and the washing machine like so many young wives nowadays. If only, Elizabeth said to herself, she doesn't do anything silly this maddening quarrel that Mark's picking with Guy . . .

Mark looked down at Hilary and didn't speak. Hilary smiled. 'Well, Master,' she said, 'I hope you're going to be in a better mood tomorrow than you were on Tuesday. I never heard such cursing; your vocabulary's growing.'

'Bastards,' said Mark without animosity. 'They galloped slap over the line. How they expect me to show sport when they override my hounds—but it's always the same when your father's not out.' He was looking at Hilary and his mind was not on his words. Hilary, who knew that, as always, some sort of stratosphere around Mark had opened and let her in, knew also that she didn't have to talk. But now nervousness drove her on.

'Scent ought to be good. We always find at Scrubs—mind you engineer a few checks; I don't want too good a day—I'm riding one of Bob's youngsters.'

'Why doesn't he ride the thing himself? Don't you go breaking your neck, Hilary. Bob's not worth it.'

'Bob's riding an even greener one. The one I'm having—the bay gelding—is supposed to be a prospective three-day-event horse. Very prospective at the moment, I'm afraid. Bob has the oddest ideas about dressage.' She knew Mark wasn't listening and suddenly he interrupted her.

'I hate these damn parties. You can't hear yourself think. I must find Clara. See you tomorrow, Hilary.'

Left alone, Hilary thought, There you are, my girl, there's no future in it. He took Clara for better or for worse and he means to stick to his bargain. He won't have an affair with you because he's friends with your parents, and the whole thing's a hellish muddle. This, she reminded herself, is what comes of letting the heart rule the head. Better go back and talk to Guy.

Mark found his wife enjoying her conversation with Bob Bewley.

'Too early, darling. Such a lovely party—haven't enjoyed myself so much for years and years,' she protested tearfully.

'It's half past seven,' her husband pointed out patiently. 'Nan's out and the children are cooking the supper. We shall catch it if we're late.'

'Mark loves the children, do anything for them, Mark would,' Clara told Bob.

'Bob loves the ladies, much better idea,' said Bob, and they both began to giggle drunkenly.

Mark persuaded his wife to leave at last and, taking an abrupt farewell of the Chadwicks, hurried her out to the car.

'Clara's a good girl,' she told him with pride. 'Only one drink. You can't say a person's a drunk who only has one drink. Jolly abstem, abstem—well, you know what I mean.'

'I know,' said Mark with a sigh. 'But God knows what you put away beforehand.'

In the Chadwicks' drawing-room everyone drew a little closer together.

'What a dreadful sight she is,' said Sonia Denton. 'I don't think he ought to take her about; she ought to be in a home. It's disgusting really, she was swaying about all over the place. I thought she'd fall down at any minute. She slopped her drink all over you, didn't she, Colonel?'

'Nearly, but not quite,' answered Douglas Holmes-Waterford. 'Fortunately I was able to avert disaster.'

'She's been in a home,' Antonia Brockenhurst told Sonia. 'About three times, I think, but it didn't do any good; she always begins again. She won't make the effort; she's just a weak character. I wonder what made her start.'

'A good servant and a bad master,' said Commander Chadwick, trying to turn the conversation to more impersonal channels.

Guy Vickers ignored his host's hint. 'I should think Broughton's dam' difficult to live with,' he said.

'No, no, you've got him entirely wrong,' objected Douglas Holmes-Waterford. 'Mark's one of my oldest friends—we were at school together. He's going through a very difficult time at present. Knowing the circumstances as I do, one can hardly blame the poor fellow for being a bit strung up.'

'I'll take your word for it,' answered Vickers carelessly. But the Colonel had already turned away to say goodbye to his hosts.

'Love to Alicia,' said Elizabeth Chadwick. 'We're so sorry she couldn't come.'

CHAPTER TWO

EVERYONE outside and inside the Dog and Duck was talking about Guy Vickers, but it was Mrs. Gordon, the licensee's wife, who brought the news to the hunt staff in their isolated splendour.

'Have you heard about poor Mr. Vickers, sir?' she asked Mark, as she made her way through the friendly, restless hounds carrying a glass of cherry brandy.

'Mr. Vickers? No.'

'He's gone. Died in the Royal Wintshire early this morning.'

'Good Lord! That was very sudden, wasn't it? He seemed all right up at Commander Chadwick's last night.'

'I don't think they know what it was yet; someone did say something about food poisoning . . .'

Mark gave her the empty glass. 'Well,' he said, 'it comes to all of us sooner or later.'

'Heard about Vickers, Master?' asked Bob Bewley, edging his way through hounds to reach Mark.

''Ware 'orse!' yelled Mark at Winsome, who was between Bob's horse's feet. 'Yes, Mrs. Gordon's just been telling me. Seems very sudden.'

'There's a rumour that they suspect dirty work at the crossroads. Anyway they're doing a P.M. He started to feel ill just after you left last night. He went out and was sick and at first we thought he'd just had one over the eight. But then he got much worse and Steve Denton didn't like the look of him at all. So they got Skindle and an ambulance and took him to the Royal Wintshire, but apparently they weren't able to do much for him there. I wish I could remember a bit more about that party. I got a bit high early on and the rest of the evening's more or less hazy.'

'Charlie coming out?' asked Mark.

'No, they were up half the night. Hilary rang me up this morning to say she couldn't ride the bay. She said they'd tried to get on to you, but you'd left.'

'Then ask Duggie to act as field master, will you? And tell him to hold those bastards up if we find at the Lindens, and give hounds a chance to get away.'

'Right you are,' said Bob, turning his horse.

Looking round, Mark saw his nephew skyed up on one of the hunt horses—he had exhausted his own pony whipping in on Tuesday.

'Uncle Mark, is the Colonel going to act as field-master?'

'I hope so.'

'Hell! Need Deb and I stay with him? He never has a clue where he is.'

'Well, can't you tell him?'

'No, he takes offence. Deb told him he was going in the opposite direction to the hounds once and he was livid.'

'It wasn't a very tactful way of putting it,' said Mark with a grin. 'Look, stay with him until we find and then come on with Frank or Alan. But remember, no jumping gates on that horse.'

13

'O.K.,' said Jon and rode away to find his sister. Mark waited until he saw Douglas Holmes-Waterford mount his horse and then blew a short note on his horn. 'Hounds, please,' he called and the milling crowds in the gravelled yard made way, and then fell in behind him, a jostling mass of excited horses that filled the road from hedge to hedge. As he drew near the Lindens he sent Frank Haines, his first whip, on to the end of the cover, signalled to Holmes-Waterford to keep the field on the road. Then he took the horn from between his coat buttons and calling to his hounds rode up over the bank into the wood.

The field were still talking about Guy Vickers.

'Poor Mrs. Chadwick, how perfectly dreadful for her.'

'But it couldn't have been the eats because the rest of 'em are as fit as fiddles; that lets the Chadwicks out.'

'It must have been something he'd eaten earlier.'

'I've heard the cook at Catton Hall is filthy.'

'Rosemary! For heaven's sake—that's slanderous.'

'Poor Guy, sickening to die at thirty-four when you've been through the war and everything.'

'Shows it's no good worrying. When your ticket's up, it's up, as my old batman used to say.'

'Perhaps he was allergic to something.'

'Doctors are such fools.'

Then they heard Mark blowing hounds out of cover and knew he had drawn the Lindens blank. Now for Scrubs Wood. Hard-riding members of the field began to grumble, for they knew it would take at least an hour to get a fox away from Scrubs, a great straggling covert intersected by boggy rides. Rides where you stood all crammed together, dripped on by trees and kicked at by other people's restive youngsters.

Brigadier Lampton, Chief Constable of Wintshire, was or of the old type, a military man appointed before it became the habit for the police to fill their own senior posts.

'I've never met Vickers myself,' he told a hastily summoned conference of Superintendent Fox and Detective Inspector Hollis of the County Constabulary. 'But I've seen him ride. Saw him win at Badminton last year—a wonderful man across country.'

Hollis wasn't listening because the Superintendent had passed him the post mortem report, but Fox murmured, 'Indeed, sir.'

'Of course, I know Commander Chadwick quite well,' Lampton went on. 'The most silent man in the silent service was what they called him, I believe. Still, his wife talks enough for two.'

'He's been most helpful, sir. We've a complete list of the guests with their approximate times of arrival and departure. We know what they drank and, in quite a number of cases, who talked to whom.'

'Jolly good work. But are we absolutely certain that the arsenic was administered at this party?'

'Well, sir, we can only go on what the experts tell us. Give us that report a minute, Hollis. Here we are, half an hour to an hour is the usual time lapse before the appearance of symptoms—in the case of a full stomach the action is delayed, but in this case the stomach was virtually empty. He was staying at Catton Hall—that residential riding school place. I understand from Commander Chadwick that there is a Continental riding expert there at the moment and that Mr. Vickers had taken the opportunity to get some advice on the training of his horses. He had been there a fortnight and had intended staying for another fortnight. We sent a man out there this morning and he interviewed the proprietors, Major and Mrs. Pierce, and the staff. The main fact which emerged from this report is that Mr. Vickers definitely spent the latter part of yesterday afternoon in the indoor riding school. At approximately five-thirty he hurried to the house to change, informing several people that he was going to be late for an appointment. He reappeared at five minutes to six—Mrs. Pierce states that the weather forecast was just coming on at that moment so the timing would appear to be accurate. He told Mrs. Pierce he would be back for dinner and according to her he seemed very cheerful. He ran downstairs and she heard his car start before she went back to listen to the news. Mr. Vickers drove a powerful sports car and, on the face of it, this time of departure would fit in with Commander Chadwick's estimated time of arrival at six-ten. All the staff at Catton Hall are most emphatic in stating that they served Mr. Vickers with no food or drink after lunch.'

'Might he have stopped for a quick one on the way?' asked the Chief Constable. 'Just a suggestion.'

'I hardly think he would have had the time, sir. But I'll see inquiries are made along the entire route. It's lucky for us there *is* only one way from Melborough to Hazebrook.'

'What about the family? You saw them this morning, didn't you?'

'I had an interview with Mr. James Vickers, the deceased's father. He was upset, naturally, but he struck me as the sort to make trouble. Questions in the House; knows somebody who knows the Home Secretary; you know the sort, sir, plenty of weight and only too willing to throw it about.'

'Yes, I know them—all too well,' said the Chief Constable with a sigh. 'But could he throw any light on the matter?'

'No, not a gleam. His son had no enemies, was in excellent health, never suffered from depression and had no monetary difficulties. The entire estate will now go to the younger brother, Paul, who is at present ski-ing in Switzerland. By the way, Hollis, we'd better check that. He wouldn't be the first lad not to be where his dad thought he was.'

'Right, sir,' answered Hollis, a burly man with a low forehead, an aggressive nose and very little chin.

'To return to the Chadwicks,' went on Fox; 'it's unfortunate that they washed up the glasses. Natural of course, because at the time they didn't suspect anything; but hearing that they had only a daily woman I had hopes of finding the washing-up piled or stacked or whatever the expression is. But, no luck. Mrs. Chadwick and her daughter had washed up by the time we got in touch with them.'

'My wife won't leave a thing, not even the saucepans,' observed the Chief Constable ruefully.

'Mrs. Fox is just the same, sir. Likes everything spick and span.'

Natter, natter, thought Hollis. Oh come on, what time do you think I'm going to get through tonight? Aloud he asked, 'Is that the lot, sir? I'd like to get on with these interviews. And with regard to the poison,' he looked at Fox, 'I think it was settled to lay on an extra man to go round the chemists, ironmongers and so on?'

'That's right,' answered Fox. 'You carry on, Hollis. You've got all the names and addresses?'

When the door closed behind Hollis the Chief Constable got to his feet and wandered round the office in an absentminded manner, humming tunes from the musical comedies of his youth. Fox, who knew from experience that this was a prelude to serious utterance, began to classify what information he had in chronological order. When the humming ceased he looked up expectantly.

'I don't like it, Fox, I don't like it at all,' said the Chief Constable turning back from the window. 'I don't think Hollis is up to it. He's never handled a murder investigation. For two pins I'd ask for help. I know he did a good job over those burglaries at Little Holt; and he got the boy who pinched the lead from the church roof at Barkly. But these Vickers' have got influence, you said so yourself, they're just the sort to raise a stink. And anyway, apart from all that, murder's murder.'

'Well, there's got to be a first time for everything, sir,' said Fox soothingly. 'And then again you never know— when we come to look into the case we may find the

18

answer's obvious. If you want my advice I should sleep on it, sir. Sleep on it, that's what I'd do.'

'I dare say you're right, Fox,' said the Chief Constable, delighted to have his mind made up for him. 'We'll see what tomorrow brings and, if Hollis isn't getting anywhere, we'll have a little talk with New Scotland Yard.'

CHAPTER THREE

DETECTIVE INSPECTOR Brian Hollis had every intention
of getting somewhere. In fact he already looked on this
case as his big chance and, as he was driven towards
Melborough Park, saw his name in the daily papers and
heard himself commended in court. I've got push and
drive, he thought, I get on with a case. Not like Fox and
the Chief Constable; there they sit, a couple of dithering
old women, chewing over every detail, seesawing over
decisions . . .

Melborough Park, a large white Georgian house, had
been partly demolished to fit it for habitation in the
twentieth century. In what remained of the house lived
Melborough's only corn merchant while the park, divided
by wire fences into a dozen rat-trap fields, was
avariciously farmed by a smallholder. The stables had
been turned into flats. In Flat 2 lived Mr. and Mrs.
Denton. Hollis's list told him that Stephen Denton was the
junior partner in the veterinary practice of Marley and
Skinner and that he had been at the Chadwicks' party
with his wife, Sonia.

Sonia Denton was alone when he arrived. 'My
husband's weekend on,' she told Hollis, her pretty, silly
face drooping with discontent. 'And animals are even less
considerate than people. They all whelp, foal or calve
from midnight onwards; they choose the weekends for
overeating, cutting themselves on barbed wire fences and
spraining their legs. And at six o'clock every Saturday

night throughout the season all the hunting people phone wanting antitetanus injections given to horses they've staked during the day.'

'Very trying, I'm sure,' said Hollis in a rudely uninterested voice. 'But since it's just a matter of a few routine questions you can probably help me. You've heard about Mr. Guy Vickers' death?'

'Yes,' answered Sonia in a small voice. 'It was horrible, so sudden—'

'We are trying to establish exactly how he spent his last evening. Now can you tell me what time you and Mr. Denton arrived at Commander Chadwick's residence?'

'About half past six, I think,' said Sonia. 'That was the time we agreed to get there. I hate to arrive early. It's so embarrassing to be first, but Steve—'

'Six-thirty,' interrupted Hollis as he entered the figure in his notebook. 'And the time of your departure?'

'It was after eight, I think. You see, with poor Guy being so ill everything became a bit disorganized and my husband, being a vet, was trying to help.'

'Yes, of course. Did you speak to Mr. Vickers at all during the evening?'

'Only just to say hello.'

'Do you know him well?'

'Fairly well, I suppose. I mean, we've met him a good many times; he comes to Catton Hall quite often, but he's rather smart for us. He's—he was I mean—very rich, and of course he's a very well-known rider.'

'Yes, I know all that. Now, did your husband speak to Mr. Vickers in the course of the party?'

'He just said good evening. That was all until Guy was taken ill. Then he talked to him a lot, in fact he stayed with him all the time until the ambulance came. I hate that sort of thing—blood and sickrooms, so sordid—but Steve doesn't mind.'

'Did you notice anyone besides Commander Chadwick touching the table on which the glasses and drinks were set out?'

'Oh no,' said Sonia in tones of horror. 'You can't mean that; you don't mean that he was deliberately poisoned? Not *murdered*. No one there would have done a thing like that.'

'You mean that you can think of no reason why any of those present should want Mr. Vickers out of the way?'

'No,' she said, and then she hesitated for a moment, 'No,' she repeated, but with less certainty. 'No, of course not. None of them would do a thing like that.'

Below a door banged. 'Oh, there's my husband,' said Sonia gratefully. She opened the sitting-room door and called down the stairs, 'Darling, there's a detective here.'

'Yes, I know, I saw his car,' a voice called back. 'I'm just washing; I won't be a second.'

A few moments later Steve Denton came bounding up the stairs.

'Sorry to keep you waiting,' he told Hollis. 'I was covered in blood—wretched cow practically cut its leg off. Darling,' he turned to his wife. 'Have we offered the Inspector a drink?'

'Not just now, thank you,' said Hollis. 'I've a few routine questions to ask you in connexion with Mr.

22

Vickers' death.'

'Was he poisoned then?' asked Steve.

'Yes, it seems probable.'

'Arsenic?'

Hollis looked at him sharply. 'What makes you think it was arsenic?'

Steve laughed. 'Don't look at me as though you were about to arrest me, Inspector. I'm a vet, you know. I didn't like the look of Vickers at all last night and there were symptoms which seemed to point to arsenical poisoning.'

'Have you any arsenic in your possession?'

'No, I haven't,' answered Steve firmly.

'Presumably you have access to it in your veterinary capacity?'

'We stock various preparations containing a negligible amount, certainly, but I doubt whether we have any in a form strong enough to do much mischief. You would have to ask George Murray about that, he does our dispensing.'

Hollis, having asked Steve for how long and how well he had known Guy Vickers and received answers which wore or less coincided with Sonia's, said sourly that he had all the information he required for the present and was shown out with alacrity.

'Nasty sort of copper,' said Steve, when he came upstairs again.

'Why *did* you have to talk about poison? Why couldn't you keep your mouth shut instead of showing off about arsenic?' demanded Sonia, her voice rising to a wail.

Steve looked at her in amazement. 'What on earth are you getting all worked up about?' he asked. 'I'm a vet, I

23

can't help using my eyes. Anyway, you only antagonize the police if you appear evasive; it's best to be perfectly open and frank with them. This is England, Sonia. You don't get clapped in jail for opening your mouth.'

'He asked me if there was anyone at the party who disliked Guy, anyone who had a *reason* for murdering him.'

Stephen looked at her for a moment and when he spoke again his voice was hard. 'Well, if I had a reason that's not my fault, is it?' he said.

Hollis read out the second name on his list; Miss Antonia Brockenhurst, Sleeches Farm, Langley. 'I know her,' Hughes, his driver, told him. 'That's where I come from, Langley. Well-known point-to-point rider, she is; won the Ladies' Race at the West Wintshire three years running. She goes all right, but she's not much to look at. Always seems as though she needs a good wash to me.'

'Well, if you know where the place is, get on with it,' said Hollis. 'We don't want to be stuck out in the wilds somewhere at midnight.'

'Right, sir,' said Hughes, offended, and did not speak again until he stopped the police car outside the square brick and flint farmhouse. Though it was growing dark, there was no light in any of the windows. 'I expect she's round in the yard,' said Hughes, thinking with relish of Hollis's light town shoes and the mud that abounded there.

The yapping of half a dozen dogs was all that greeted the Inspector's knock on the front door, but he persisted until a voice from the farmyard called, 'It's no good knocking; there's no one there. You'll have to come on round.'

Swearing under his breath he squelched round to the farmyard. In the barn was a tall young woman, wearing an old dufflecoat over hunting kit, filling haynets by the light of a hurricane lantern.

'Miss Antonia Brockenhurst?' he asked.

'Yes, that's right.'

'I'm a police officer making a few inquiries in connexion with the death of Mr. Guy Vickers. I believe you were at Commander Chadwick's cocktail party last night.'

'Yes, that's right.'

Antonia Brockenhurst needed no prodding back to the point; she answered Hollis's questions as briefly as he could wish. She hadn't noticed the time of her arrival at the Chadwicks,' but Mr. Vickers had been waiting on the doorstep and they had been let in together. Only Captain Bewley and the Chadwicks themselves were there before her. She hadn't spoken to Vickers except on the doorstep. So far as she knew there was no arsenic on the farm, certainly no weedkiller; she and her partner didn't bother with the garden, they just turned the puppies loose in it. But when Hollis asked her if she knew whether Vickers had any enemies or if there was anyone who might have a reason for wishing him out of the way, after saying she hadn't a clue, she seemed to hesitate.

'Well?' said Hollis sharply.

'No, it's too silly. People don't murder for that sort of

thing.'

'I'm the one to decide that,' Hollis told her.

'But it's too silly, really. It's just that Colonel Clinkerton, the hunt secretary, told me that the Master, that's Mr Broughton, and Mr. Vickers had had a terrific row. Someone had suggested that if they made Mr. Vickers joint master the hunt would have enough money. The subscriptions keep falling and Mr. Broughton can't afford to put up any more; they've got to economize and the committee don't like it.'

'And Mr. Broughton didn't approve of the suggestion?'

'No, not according to Colonel Clinkerton.'

Hollis asked for the Colonel's address and then, snapping his notebook shut, thanked her briefly. As he squelched from the yard he reflected that at least he had something to compensate him for shivering in a barn with frozen, mud-soaked feet. Back in the comparative comfort of the car, he turned to Hughes.

'Do you know Hazebrook? We want Captain Robert Bewley.'

'Ah, you want the Captain, do you, sir? Bit of a lad 'e is,' said Hughes and then, remembering he was offended, added sullenly: 'It's 'alfway back to Melborough and turn off left.'

Bob Bewley was covered in mud. He had taken a purler, he explained, his youngster having failed to stand off a solid post and rails. 'Still, it learned him,' said Bewley with a grin. 'He jumped the next one a treat.'

Hollis, having no wish to listen to hunting experiences, cut him short with a question about his time of arrival at the Chadwicks' party, but Bewley did not answer it. 'Come along inside,' he said, turning out the saddle-room light. 'I've given the horses some grub so they'll do for a bit. Let's get out of this dam' wind and have a drink.'

The Inspector followed him through a back door surrounded by overflowing dustbins into a small kitchen where a couple of Jack Russells gave them an enthusiastic welcome. Bewley cleared the table of empty bottles, dirty crockery and an overflowing ashtray which he piled on the floor by the sink.

'Sorry about the mess,' he said. 'My wife left me a couple of weeks ago—took the fridge too—since then I've been fending for myself.'

'Fending's about the word,' remarked Hollis, looking round disapprovingly.

Bewley laughed. 'I'm better in the stable,' he said. 'Drink? Big Brother isn't looking. I prefer it pure and undiluted,' he added as he poured out two tots of whisky, but there's the tap if you like it that way. Good hunting.' He drank.

Hollis smacked his lips. 'Helps to keep the cold out,' he said appreciatively, producing his notebook and pencil.

'I heard a rumour that there'd been dirty work at the crossroads last night, I suppose your appearance means it's true?' Bewley poured himself out another drink.

'Just a routine inquiry,' answered Hollis, and began his questions.

Bewley had been the first of the Chadwicks' guests to arrive. 'I'd only a mile to go and I'm always thirsty, Inspector,' he explained. 'I suppose I got there about five past six and I talked to the Chadwicks until Vickers and Miss Brockenhurst came. Vickers took Miss Chadwick into a corner. I think he thought the rest of us were a bit beneath him. We talked shop—hunting, horses.'

He knew of no reason why anyone should wish to murder Guy Vickers.

'But who gets the dough?' he asked. 'I believe there's plenty of it. Anyway you can count me out, Inspector. I was all set to sell him a horse—I've got the very thing for Badminton and I'd have had a good price out of Vickers too. I'd even got Hilary Chadwick lined up to ride the brute—knew Vickers couldn't be off seeing it if *she* was on top.'

Hollis brought him briskly back to the point with a question about arsenic. 'No,' Bewley said, 'no arsenic. Unless,' he added flippantly, 'my old woman bought some to do me in with. But I reckon rat poison was more in her line—she had a very low opinion of hubby. Never mind, she's happy now with Mother and the fridge.'

'Just one more query,' said Hollis. 'You sound as though you were well up in hunt matters—what do you make of this quarrel between Mr. Vickers and Mr. Broughton?'

'Quarrel?'

'You haven't heard about it, then?'

'Not about a quarrel. I'd heard that some member of the committee had suggested that they might get the hunt finances out of a sticky mess by taking on a joint master with some dough, and that Mark Broughton had said he'd rather cut down expenditure—which of course he's a perfect right to do.'

'But no quarrel?' persisted Hollis, about to pocket his notebook.

'No quarrel,' repeated Bob Bewley. 'Hellish dark and smells of cheese,' he added, opening the door for the detective. 'But perhaps it's only the dustbins. Come again, Inspector. Any time—always glad to see you.'

'Good night, sir,' said Hollis, in tones a shade less surly than usual, and getting into the car told Hughes to drive him to Lapworth Manor.

' 'Alfway back to Melborough. Turn again, Whittington,' said Hughes uppishly, emboldened by the knowledge that his superior had been drinking on duty.

CHAPTER FOUR

DUGGIE HOLMES-WATERFORD had lost hounds early in the afternoon. Riding round the countryside with an embarrassing following of some thirty horsemen, he had suffered all the pangs of humiliation in silence and without sign. The surreptitious searching for hoofprints in muddy gateways, the scorn of farm labourers, the mortification of consulting little boys, all the indignities of the lost were heaped upon him and magnified by his scarlet coat and top hat, his magnificent horse, his air and position of authority. With mixed feelings he had watched his field dwindle, shorn of defiant little groups who had decided they would do better without a field master and a trickle of individuals who had given up the day as a bad job and turned for home.

At three o'clock, Holmes-Waterford decided that he himself had had enough, and having apologized rather stiffly to what remained of his following took the road for Lapworth. Alone, he was able to measure the disaster. He had lost hounds, it was true, but one must not reckon without the contributory factors. Mark was a first class amateur huntsman, but even the best are not without fault and in these great woodland coverts he was too silent, much too silent . . . As for the country, it was fast becoming unrideable; he had defied anyone to keep with hounds over a country intersected by four-foot-six barbed wire fences. Something would have to be done; a thousand pounds laid out on hunt jumps would be well spent. It was a pity about Vickers. They could have done with some more money in the hunt coffers. Poor old Mark liked to crow on his own dunghill, couldn't make room for two kings on the castle. Still, it was a pity, for Mark, tactfully handled, might have seen sense.

He came to Lapworth and turned up the long straight drive to the Manor. Facing him, the triple-gabled house of dark red Elizabethan brick, stood stately among its lawns and yew hedges. It was a sight that always brought him solace and satisfaction, if not happiness.

Philby was waiting to take the horse in the stableyard. 'Had a good day, sir?' The Colonel shook his head. 'Rotten,' he said, 'but the horse went well. He's taken nothing out of himself, I may ride him again on Tuesday.' From the immaculately kept yard he entered the house by a side door. Gold met him in the hall.

'Madam's not back yet, sir. Will you have tea in the library?'

'Yes, but give me five minutes to get my boots off.'

The library was officially his particular room. It was true that few of the books either belonged to or had been read by him, that the furniture, even to his desk, had been chosen by Alicia Holmes-Waterford's pet antique dealer; but the effect was pleasing, if formal, and as a sop to comfort he had been allowed two leather-covered armchairs in which the dogs—two middle-aged Labradors—were now comfortably ensconced. A log fire blazed in the grate and the curtains were drawn against the night.

'Come on, Pluto, out of it,' said Duggie. 'Where's master

to sit?' In possession of his chair, he turned to the table beside him. A tea tray, the twelve o'clock post, *The Times* and *Horse and Hound* awaited him.

Arriving some two hours later, Hollis caught only a glimpse of the house and grounds in the car's headlights, but what he saw told him that the place was well kept. As he waited for a few moments in the panelled hall a glance round confirmed his impression that there was money and to spare. Temporarily overawed, his manner became servile.

Colonel Holmes-Waterford was reasonably certain that he had got to the Chadwicks' at six-fifteen. He had looked at his watch before getting out of his car and, finding himself on the early side, had been glad to see that there were already several cars parked in the road. He thought that Miss Brockenhurst, Mr. Vickers, Captain Bewley and, of course, the Chadwicks had been there when he arrived. The Dentons had arrived after him and the Broughtons last of all. He thought that he had spoken to almost everyone—just a word or two to some of them, but with Mr. Broughton and Commander Chadwick he had had quite lengthy conversations, mostly about hunt matters. He'd also had a chat with Mr. Vickers about his Olympic prospects. Having ridden for England himself, he explained to Hollis, he had been able to advise Vickers on several matters.

'Quite so, sir,' said Hollis. 'And as far as you know, sir, he had no enemies?'

'None at all, I should say. He always seemed a very likeable sort of lad to me. Of course I know nothing of his private life; the only thing I *have* heard is that he was a hit of a lady's man and that there were one or two husbands who didn't care for him. But that's only the veriest hearsay.'

'Quite sir,' said Hollis. 'And then there was this quarrel between Mr. Broughton and Mr. Vickers. Something to do with the hunt, I believe?'

Holmes-Waterford's laugh sounded a little hollow. 'Well, well, Inspector,' he said, 'I see you've got your ear to the ground. Still, I recommend you not to set too much store by anything you may have heard about that: the whole thing's been grossly exaggerated. You know how it is in these country places, precious little happens and so the gossips have to do their best with what little they can find. Broughton's one of my oldest friends; he's not perhaps the easiest man in the world to get on with, but you couldn't have a better fellow at heart. Of course old Colonel Clinkerton, the hunt secretary, went and rubbed him up the wrong way over this joint master business; if only he'd left it to me—still, it wouldn't be much use now.'

Hollis, who had been writing rapidly, made polite, agreeing noises and asked about arsenic. The Colonel confessed with a smile that he didn't take much interest in the garden, but that considering the absence of weeds in the paths he supposed they must use some sort of weedkiller. 'You'd better have a word with Wilson, Inspector. He has a flat over the garage.'

Hollis, dispatched across the yard with Gold as a reluctant and shivering guide, found Wilson deeply engrossed in a television programme and none too pleased at being brought back to reality. However, he readily admitted to the possession of a large quantity of arsenical weedkiller.

'I keeps it down in the potting shed,' he explained. 'I suppose you can 'ave it if 'e says so; but mind you, it's 'er who pays the wages 'ere. 'Alf a minute, while I puts on my shoes.'

Mark Broughton, wearing a white kennel coat over his hunting kit, leaned against the wall of the feed yard and watched his tired hounds at the trough. It had been the hell of a day. Hunting hounds was really no job for the master, he thought. Be an amateur huntsman by all means, but not a sort of unholy duality. It turned you against your subscribers for one thing; men you liked well enough in the ordinary way became bloody fools who overrode your hounds, stood about, got in the way and could do no right. Today, for instance, he could cheerfully have killed old Duggie, who'd been *leading* the field on those aimless perambulations round the covert which had always coincided with the fox's attempts to break. His reflections were interrupted by the appearance of Jonathan and Deborah in the feed yard. They had changed from their hunting kit and were wearing corduroy trousers, gumboots and dufflecoats.

'Uncle Mark, Bob's just rung up,' Jon told him. 'He says Guy Vickers *was* murdered. He said he'd just had a detective to see him, and he thought we'd be having him round here next.'

34

'Well, he won't eat us,' said Mark calmly, for he thought he detected a note of alarm in the boy's voice.

'Bob says that they think he was murdered by someone at the Chadwicks' party and . . .' Jon looked at his feet 'and he says someone's told the police that you kicked up about having Vickers as joint master. Bob said he'd banged down hard on that idea, but that he thought it might help if you knew which way they were running.'

Mark laughed. 'It sounds as though I'm suspect number one. Where the devil have Frank and Alan got to? If they don't hurry up I shall be arrested before I've had my tea.'

The front door of the Broughton's house at Little Lapworth was opened to Hollis by a small plump woman in her sixties. She eyed him suspiciously and then, hearing his business, showed him to an untidy sitting-room. Hollis, looking round with hard pale eyes, observed that the books had overflowed the bookcase, that the writing-desk could no longer contain its owner's correspondence, that the chimneypiece was crowded with dusty invitation cards to events long past. Untidy lot, he thought, remembering the unused splendour of the Manor House.

In the holidays the Broughtons had dining-room tea, which on hunting days was supplemented by boiled eggs. To Jonathan and Deborah's consternation, Mark insisted on finishing his egg before going to see the Inspector in the sitting-room. He took his cup of tea with him and offered the Inspector one.

'No thank you,' said Hollis. 'Not just now, I've no time to waste. I want to ask you a few routine questions in connection with the death of Mr. Guy Vickers.'

At first Mark was a model witness. He answered briefly and briskly that he and his wife had arrived at the Chadwicks' at about six-thirty. He thought they were the last arrivals. He had seen no one tampering with the glasses. He had talked to his hosts and to Colonel Holmes-Waterford, and he had had a word with Captain Bewley.

'You didn't speak to Mr. Vickers?' asked Hollis.

'No.'

'Why not?'

'Talking to all one's fellow guests isn't compulsory.'

'Were you on friendly terms with Mr. Vickers?'

'No.'

'On terms of hostility then?'

'No, I just disliked the man.'

'Why?'

'I don't need a *reason* to dislike people, I just dislike them—it happens quite often.'

'I was given to understand that you had a definite reason for disliking Mr. Vickers.'

'Other people always know one's reasons better than one does oneself,' said Mark carelessly.

'I understand that you quarrelled with Mr. Vickers over a hunt matter,' said Hollis. 'Now when and where did this quarrel take place?'

'It didn't,' answered Mark.

'You deny that there was any disagreement between you and Mr. Vickers over the hunt?'

In weary tones Mark said: 'Look, Vickers was supposed to have been lobbying members of the hunt committee

36

with a suggestion that I should take him into joint mastership. He certainly went to the hunt secretary with some sort of a proposition, heavily baited with an offer of funds—'

'In fact you did quarrel with him,' interrupted Hollis.

'No, I limited myself to telling the secretary and various other members of the committee exactly what I thought of the plan. No doubt they passed it on in due course.'

'You expect me to believe that, though you were quarrelling with Mr. Vickers on a matter of importance to you both, you didn't communicate your views to him either in person or in writing?'

'No,' said Mark. 'I mean, yes. I *do* expect you to believe that I *didn't* communicate. Look,' he went on, suddenly exasperated, 'I've told you that I didn't quarrel with Vickers and that's that. If you would stop meandering round and round the bloody point and get on with your questions I'd be grateful. You said you had no time to waste. Well, I've even less.'

'I should like to see Mrs. Broughton,' said Hollis stiffly.

'I'm sorry,' Mark told him, 'but that is impossible.'

'Impossible?' Hollis raised his bushy eyebrows. 'That's a strong word to use. On what grounds is it *impossible* to see Mrs. Broughton?'

'Well,' Mark said, more pacifically, 'if you did see her it wouldn't do you any good. To be quite frank she wasn't in very good form when she got to that misbegotten party, and I don't suppose she remembers anything about it.'

'I should like to form my own opinion on the matter,' said Hollis coldly.

Mark flung open the door and yelled *'Nan,'* into the hall.

'Now what is it?' The answer seemed to float sourly down from somewhere upstairs. Mark ignored it and soon the grey-haired woman who had let Hollis in, appeared.

'This policeman wants to see Mrs. Broughton,' Mark told her.

'Well, you know very well he can't,' she said fiercely. 'Not for all the policemen in England will I open her door.' She turned on Hollis. 'If you want to talk to her you come back tomorrow. She might be better then—if Mr. Broughton stays at home,' she added, with a spiteful look at Mark.

'Very well.' Hollis's voice was cold. 'And I'll trouble you for the name of the lady's doctor.'

'Dr. Skindle,' said Nan. 'Mrs. Broughton's always gone to him ever since she come to this 'ouse.'

'Now,' said Hollis when he had entered the doctor's name in his notebook. 'Have you any poisons in your possession? I'm thinking especially of arsenic, which many households keep in the form of a weedkiller.'

'God knows what we've got,' answered Mark. 'Codding does the garden so you'd better ask him about the weedkiller. Miss Hatch here looks after the human medicine chest and Philips, the stud groom, is in charge of the horse one. Haines, the first whip and kennel huntsman, has enough hound remedies over at the kennels to poison an army.'

'There's no arsenic in my cupboard,' said Nan firmly. 'I don't believe in keeping no poisons about, only

38

camphorated oil for Deborah's chest when she gets that terrible cough of hers—I moistens the cotton wool with it, just like old Dr. Canning said.'

'All right, Nan,' Mark said. 'No one's accusing you of anything.'

'I should think not,' Nan told him indignantly. *I've* done nothing to get mixed up with the police. Thirty years I worked for her ladyship and never a word of complaint. I've never been used to the sort of houses where the police come with their poking and prying—'

'Miss Hatch,' said Hollis sternly, 'a crime has been committed and it is the duty of every citizen to help the police in their investigations.' He turned to Mark. 'Is the man who does the gardening available?'

'Codding? Yes, I expect so.' Mark looked at his watch. 'He has a room over the stables, he'll be there unless he's gone to the local. I'll come across with you.'

'That won't be necessary. I saw the stables as I came in.'

'Oh. All right—but Codding's an elderly man and not very easy to handle.'

'In the police we are trained to handle *all* sorts without assistance,' said Hollis.

'Very well, Inspector. Then perhaps you'll let me get on with my work?'

'I may require additional information when I've seen Codding,' remarked Hollis unpleasantly, and in the tone of one who holds the whip hand.

Mark, who had been keeping his temper with difficulty, left the room without another word.

'A very disagreeable man,' said Nan as the door closed

behind him. 'A very disagreeable man indeed. If it hadn't been for her I'd have given in my notice many a time. Those children aren't much better either—ungrateful little things.'

Hollis seized his opportunity. 'Well, Miss Hatch,' he said. Perhaps you can help me. Do you know anything about this hunt quarrel?'

'Quarrel? They're always a-quarrelling. Mr. Broughton would quarrel with that wall. Mud all over his clothes, mud all over the house and all his time spent out there in them stables. There she is, left alone day in, day out; but she won't have a word against him—not a word.'

'Quite,' said Hollis. 'But it's facts I want. Well, I won't waste any more time. I'll go and see this Codding.'

'You won't get nothing out of him, he's a regular old fool.' Nan gave a contemptuous sniff. 'Thinks the world of Mr. Broughton, Codding does. Can't see no further than the end of his nose.'

Since the death of his wife, seven years before, Fred Codding had made the avoidance of draughts the prime purpose of his existence. From his little garret above the forage rooms all air was rigorously excluded. At Hollis's knock he extricated himself from shawl and rug, rose stiffly from his chair beside the oil stove and freed the door from its thick fustian curtain and the roll of newspaper which guarded the crack below. Looking like an elderly tortoise, he peered out at Hollis, who was momentarily overcome by the blast of hot air and the reek of oil which met him.

'Weedkiller?' repeated Codding stupidly, when Hollis

had stated his business. 'Weedkiller? Whatever do the police want that for? There's no law against 'aving weedkiller.'

'It's none of your business what we want it for; but it's in connection with a murder inquiry. Now have you any weedkiller?'

'Perhaps I 'ave and perhaps I 'aven't. We'll 'ave to go down to the shed to see. Come on in and shut that door, while I gets my overcoat. I don't want this room like an ice 'ouse.'

'It's more like an oven,' said Hollis, looking round with a disparaging eye.

'I can't stand draughts, I can't. Only got to sit in one a couple of minutes and I gets a terrible pain all down my leg. Sciatica, Dr. Skindle reckons it is, but 'e don't seem able to do nothing for it.'

Hollis ignored the old man's chatter as he followed him across the stableyard, through a wicker gate and down a gravelled path between box hedges. The bitterness of the wind seemed to have increased and it whipped round the garden, tearing at the frozen hedges and the rows of stiff, bedraggled brussels sprouts. Codding fumbled with the door of the potting shed which opened at last with a creak and a groan. He shone his torch on a shelf cluttered with paint pots, some half full, some empty. Hollis added his more powerful beam. Slowly the old man put up a shaking hand, shifted a few pots, and then, one by one, lifted them down until the shelf was bare. Now his face looked grey and a little frightened as he turned to the detective. ' 'E's gone!' he said. That's where I keeps 'im. Someone's 'ad 'im.'

CHAPTER FIVE

HOLLIS, himself an aggressive agnostic, was afraid that he would find the Chadwicks at church when he drove through the village of Hazebrook on Sunday morning and heard the bells and saw a considerable part of the population converging on the church, just visible from the road through the boughs of the frost-rimed trees. However, he found such of the family as he wanted at home. Hilary, boyish in corduroys and sweater, was mucking out the two horses; Elizabeth Chadwick's head called 'Good morning,' from the kitchen window and the commander appeared round the corner of the cottage carrying a basket of logs. They seemed pleased to see Hollis; abandoning their occupations, they ushered him into the drawing-room, where a newly-lit fire burned feebly.

'Any news?' asked Elizabeth Chadwick.

'The investigation is proceeding satisfactorily,' Hollis told her.

'Does that mean that you *do* suspect someone?' asked Charlie Chadwick.

'We've narrowed down the field a good deal. More than that I'm not at liberty to tell you.'

'I don't see who you *can* suspect,' objected Hilary. 'At least not among the people who were at the party.'

'Well, you're hardly trained in police work, miss, so perhaps you wouldn't know where to begin.'

'I don't believe that it was murder at all,' said Mrs.

42

Chadwick. 'Superintendent Fox said it was arsenic that killed Guy. Well, look at the people who get poisoned by it quite accidentally. There was that woman diplomat, she absorbed it from a ceiling, and there was a man who got it off the greens playing golf. Has anyone tested the ceilings at Catton Hall? That's what I want to know. The police are going to look silly if they hold a full scale murder inquiry and then it turns out that all they needed was a little common sense.'

'The police are quite capable of conducting a murder enquiry, madam,' said Hollis coldly, and Charlie Chadwick, trying to keep the peace, added—'My dear Elizabeth, neither of your examples took a lethal dose of arsenic. As far as I remember, they suffered from repeated bouts of sickness and vague pains and cramps. Poor Guy was in perfect health one minute and dead the next.'

'In any case,' said Hollis, 'we have discovered the absence of a tin of arsenical poison and it seems possible that the murderer had access to it.'

'Oh,' Elizabeth sounded shocked, 'then you mean we really have got a murderer in our midst?' And she began to search among her acquaintances for a suspect.

'I still don't believe it was anyone at the party,' said Hilary. 'It couldn't have been.' She turned to Hollis. 'Do you think someone could have doctored Guy's glucose tablets? He was always eating them for extra energy and everyone knew that he did.'

Elizabeth said, 'There you are, Inspector, there's a suggestion and it sounds much more likely than your theory that one of our guests poisoned Mr. Vickers.'

43

'Who's minus their weedkiller, Inspector?' asked her husband. 'Or is that still on the secret list?'

Hollis's irritation at the chatter suddenly burst forth.

'I would like to ask you a few questions, Commander,' he snapped. 'Is there another room available?'

Chadwick nodded. 'Yes, of course. We'll go into the dining-room.'

'What a *horrible* 'tec,' said Elizabeth as the door closed behind the two men. 'I much prefer Superintendent Fox and those funny constables we had yesterday; not that they seemed the least likely to solve anything.'

Hilary mused. 'I wonder whom he suspects? Isn't it a horrible thought that one of those people may have murdered Guy? But I don't believe it; none of them had a reason.' She stood for a few moments fiddling with the ornaments on the chimneypiece and then she said, 'Well, if he doesn't want me I'll go and finish mucking out.'

Elizabeth looked after her anxiously. Did her daughter love Guy, or didn't she? she wondered. Do other people's children confide in them?

Hollis said, 'Now, sir, you gave the Superintendent a very full report of this party, but there are one or two points I should like to clear up. Mr. Broughton, for instance. You state that he stayed by the door throughout the party and didn't speak to Mr. Vickers who kept to the fireplace end of the room.'

'Quite correct,' said Chadwick.

'Rather unusual behaviour, wasn't it?'

'No, not really. Mr. Broughton isn't what they call a socialite.'

'He stood close to the table on which the wines, spirits, etc., were set out?'

'Well, the glasses were set out there and some of the food, but I was carrying round the cocktail shaker and the sherry decanter most of the time.'

'Mr. Broughton didn't help you at all?'

'No.'

'No one helped you to dispense the drinks? Not even your wife and daughter?'

'No, I'm not a great conversationalist and I like to have something to do at these parties. So, unless my son happens to be at home, I deal with the drinks and my wife and daughter look after the introductions and the things to eat.'

'I see. Now what was your opinion of Mrs. Broughton's state?'

'She seemed much the same as she has been for the last few years. I imagine you've been told that she drinks.'

Hollis grunted noncommittally. 'Yes. Mr. Broughton was evasive about it, but I gathered that much.'

'She's been in and out of homes a good deal, I believe, but they don't seem able to help her. Very sad.'

'I wonder that she attends parties if that's the way of it,' said Hollis. 'It must be embarrassing for the other guests.'

'Embarrassing for the hosts too, sometimes,' said Chadwick ruefully. 'But, when you've known people a long time you have to accept their changing fortunes. A lot of people *have* dropped them, though, and they never go to large parties. We usually ask them when we're just having a few friends.'

'I see. Now about this hunt quarrel. Mr. Vickers was in the wrong, I understand; but presumably he would have been made welcome by a large number of hunt supporters, due to the fact that he was a wealthy man?'

Commander Chadwick took out his case and lit another cigarette before he answered. Then he said: 'This "hunt quarrel" as you call it, was a molehill, Inspector. You can't make a mountain out of it. Mr. Broughton was annoyed with Mr. Vickers, but he was top dog. He's done too much for the hunt for there to be any likelihood of the committee going against his wishes. He's lived for the pack since he took it over. There was hardly a hound worth having after the war and he's built up a pack that would do the Shires credit.'

'I see,' said Hollis. 'Now, Commander, in your statement you say that you saw only Miss Chadwick, Mrs. Broughton and Colonel Holmes-Waterford actually talking to Mr. Vickers. But did you at any time see anyone near enough to slip anything into his glass?'

'Nasty question,' said Charlie Chadwick. 'Well, obviously, my wife, my daughter and myself had the most opportunity. At the beginning of the evening, when there were only a few of us, we were closer together and so I suppose either Antonia Brockenhurst or Bob Bewley might have had a chance. Apart from that, I wouldn't like to say.'

'But you are still of the opinion that Mr. Broughton never approached Mr. Vickers at any time?'

'Yes.'

'Thankyou. Now I'd like to see Mrs. Chadwick for a few

minutes.'

'I'll fetch her.'

Elizabeth Chadwick, used to fighting the domestic battles of the world from a column in one of the glossier magazines for women, was not to be intimidated by a policeman of Hollis's calibre. Under his handling she soon became contentious. No, she hadn't been watching her guests with lynx-like eyes. She had no more expected them to murder each other than she had expected them to steal the silver. She had watched for the empty hand in order to offer it an eatable, but hadn't registered to whom the hand belonged. She had watched for signs of boredom and for people with no one to talk to, but they had been few, for everyone had known everyone else.

Yes, it was true that her daughter had talked to Guy Vickers and probably for the greater part of the evening. The young people had been friendly for some time; in fact, during the party they had arranged to go out together on Saturday night. 'An understanding?' Hollis had asked, but Elizabeth was not to be drawn. If there *was* anything they had kept it to themselves.

'Has Miss Chadwick any other admirers?' asked Hollis. 'Could her friendship with Mr. Vickers have been causing jealousy in other quarters?'

'No, I don't think so. And certainly not among our guests that night,' Elizabeth answered without the tremor of an eyelid.

Hollis said, 'I'd better have a word with the young lady herself. If she knew Mr. Vickers well she may be able to throw some new light on the matter.'

47

'I don't think so,' said Elizabeth, 'but I'll see if I can find her for you; she thought you didn't want her so she's gone back to the stables.' And she left the room, hoping that Hilary had vanished on some expedition.

'Oh, Charlie, he wants to talk to Hilary now,' she said, finding her husband standing at the drawing-room window.

'She's mucking out; shall I fetch her?'

'I don't see why he has to ask her all these sordid questions. We've answered them already; why should Hilary be involved?'

'She was there and she's not a child. You needn't worry, she's taking it all very calmly.'

Men never understand, thought Elizabeth. They don't feel this desire to protect and spare, they don't realize that it goes on and on long after one's children are grown-up.

Hilary joined Hollis in the dining-room.

'Just a few questions, miss.' He spoke with a snap, not caring for her casual dress, her air of assurance or the tang of the stable which came in with her. 'I understand that you were friendly with Mr. Vickers, so no doubt you'll be anxious to help me in every way you can. I want you to think back to Friday night. First of all can you remember whether Mr. Vickers held his glass in his hand while you were talking to him or whether he put it down on some table?'

Hilary screwed up her face in an effort to recapture the scene. 'I'm almost certain he held it,' she answered. 'If he put it down it would have been on the chimneypiece— there were no tables near enough. But I'm almost sure he held it.'

'I see. Now, you talked to Mr. Vickers right from the commencement of the party until when?'

'Until Mrs. Broughton came to speak to him. I knew that I was neglecting the other guests and had a guilty conscience about it; so I seized the opportunity and fled.'

'I see, and to whom did you speak next?'

'To Mr. Broughton.'

'Oh, he was close at hand then?'

'No, he was at the other end of the room. But I could see he had no one to talk to so, naturally, I went across.'

'And for how long did you remain in conversation with him?'

'Not very long. Not more than about five minutes, anyway. Then he said he must find his wife and go.'

'And so he went across to his wife, who was talking to Mr. Vickers,' said Hollis, unable to keep a gleam out of his eyes.

'No, she'd stopped talking to him. Mr. Vickers was talking to Colonel Holmes-Waterford. I don't know where Mrs. Broughton was, I didn't see her.'

'But Mr. Broughton walked round the room looking for his wife,' insisted Hollis.

'I didn't notice,' said Hilary, conscious that she was being pushed into something.

'Well then, we'll say that he left his position by the door?'

'Yes,' she admitted reluctantly.

'Thank you, miss,' said Hollis, shutting his notebook. "That'll be all for now.'

When Hollis had gone they compared notes.

'He's gunning for Mark all right,' said Charlie Chadwick. 'I imagine they've lost the weedkiller at the kennels and the motive is what the Inspector calls "the hunt quarrel". Too ridiculous. As if Mark or anyone else, would murder for that.'

'Just how silly can the police get?' asked Elizabeth. 'Really, you know, they're only fit to hound motorists; no wonder there are so many unsolved crimes. Anyway I didn't tell him much, I still think it's those ceilings at Catton Hall.'

Her husband laughed, 'I foxed him,' he said. 'I swore that Mark never moved from the door.'

Hilary looked uneasy. 'I'm afraid he was cleverer with me. I had to give a recital of all my conversations and unfortunately it ended with Mark saying that he must go and find his wife.'

'Oh dear,' said Elizabeth. 'But he didn't go near Guy, did he?'

'Well, actually, he did, but I had the sense not to admit that.'

'Don't perjure yourself for Mark,' Chadwick said gravely. 'Remember, he's innocent until he's proved guilty. Don't risk even white lies to the police.'

'How can one tell the truth to a bone-headed copper like that?' demanded Elizabeth. 'He's determined to put the wrong construction on everything—far better keep one's mouth shut.'

CHAPTER SIX

WHEN HOLLIS had announced that the weedkiller was missing from the potting shed Mark had taken it calmly.

'Codding's probably put it in some safe place and forgotten about it,' he said. 'Or he's finished the stuff and thrown the tin away, or he's loaned it to Philips for the stableyard. I can think of a dozen more likely fates for it than that it should have been used to poison Vickers.'

'I've no doubt *you* can,' said Hollis. 'I take it that you've nothing to add to what you've told me already, Mr. Broughton?'

'Any further comment would be unprintable,' Mark replied, and that had ended the interview. Later, he had talked to Codding and found the old man unshakable in the conviction that he had seen the weedkiller on the shelf in the potting shed only the previous Wednesday.

'Philips was carrying on 'ow someone 'ad 'ad 'is 'oof oil brush,' Codding explained. 'That's 'im all over. 'E's never lost nothing. No, someone's always 'ad it. To stop 'is moaning I said I'd get 'im an old paintbrush, and down to the shed I went and got one from the jar I keeps on the shelf. I 'ad to move things round a bit to get at the turpentine—I wanted to give it a bit of a clean up and then I sees the weedkiller. Ah, I thought, I'd forgotten I 'ad you. Come in 'andy in the spring, that will. Gave me a turn, it did, to find it gone. And now that detective's locked up my shed and took the key, so 'ow I'm to get on with the gardening I don't know.'

After that Mark had retired to the office, a bleak little room where he was supposed to keep the hunt correspondence and interview earth stoppers and gamekeepers, and had opened a bottle of whisky.

On Sunday morning he had wakened with a thick head and a bad temper. Finding two silent and apprehensive looking children wandering aimlessly about the house he had decided that their religious education was being neglected and packed them off to church. Then he'd walked round the stables, sworn at Philips for failing to report the bran supply was running low, and found fault with half a dozen details in the kennels, before returning to the office and a new bottle. By Sunday afternoon he looked ten years older than he had the previous day.

Oho, thought Hollis when he and Hughes were shown into the office by Nan, You're rattled, you are. I'll soon have you where I want you. And he began without preliminaries:

'Mr. Broughton,' he said in a hectoring voice, 'yesterday you gave me to understand that you never approached Mr. Vickers at Commander Chadwick's party. Now, from information received, I find that this statement not to accord with the facts.'

'If you mean it's a bloody lie, why don't you say so?' asked Mark and poured himself out another drink.

'I put it to you, Mr. Broughton, that the sequence of events could have been as follows: when you attended the Commander's party you had already formed a resolve to kill Mr. Vickers should the chance present itself. You therefore took with you a solution prepared from the weedkiller and, when you told Miss Chadwick that you must go and find your wife, walked round the room, waited until Mr. Vickers, who was talking to Colonel Holmes-Waterford, put his glass down in a convenient spot (probably the mantelpiece), and then introduced the solution. Well, what have you to say to that?' he asked, when Mark remained irritatingly silent.

'Are you charging me with murder?' Mark asked quietly.

'No, not at this stage.'

'Well then, I find your manner extremely offensive. I refuse to answer any more questions except in the presence of my solicitor, and I would be grateful if you'd get out of my house.'

Hollis began, 'It is the duty of every citizen . . .'

'Ah, yes,' said Mark. 'But you've just told me you think I'm a murderer. I've asked you to leave,' he added.

'Very well,' said Hollis. He left the office, but not the house. With Hughes at his heels he went to the kitchen to look for Nan. She was putting the kettle on and she signalled to them to come in and to shut the door. When she spoke it was in a conspiratorial whisper.

'One drinking upstairs and one drinking downstairs,' she said. 'Never in all my life have I been in such an 'ouse. I can't do nothing with Mrs. Broughton today. She'll 'ave that D.T. again before we know where we are and then she'll be back in one of them 'omes.' She drew closer to Hollis. 'I 'eard *'im* last night. He was asking her what she'd done with the arsenic. All night long he was looking for it. All her drawers were upside down this morning where he'd been through them. "Where's that arsenic, Clara?" he kept saying, "Where have you put it?" We're none of us safe; not with that arsenic in the 'ouse. He might take it into 'is head to kill any of us. I'm not touching anything that's been in the dining-room, that I'm not.'

'This is very interesting, Miss Hatch,' said Hollis. 'Hughes, have you got that down?'

'Yes, sir.'

'Now Miss Hatch, you're sure of the exact words? Mr. Broughton said, "Where's that arsenic, Clara? Where have you put it?" '

'That's right, and I could hear him opening all the drawers and cupboards.'

'Well, keep your ears open,' said Hollis. 'You may hear something else of interest to us. Come on, Hughes. Don't waste time. We must get back to the station.'

Jon and Deborah were hanging about in the hall. White-faced and anxious they looked beseechingly at Hollis, but he hurried by; children were people of little importance in his eyes. Sadly they returned to the sitting-room and joined the dogs round the fire. The bottom seemed to have fallen out of their world. It had happened to them once before when they had learnt that a Mau-Mau gang had murdered their parents in Kenya, but then, mercifully, they had been younger; old enough to feel the loss, but not to suffer the torment of their imaginations.

When they had come to live with their uncle and aunt at Lapworth they had accepted Clara and her gin bottle with the uncensoriousness of the unprompted child and soon Mark had somehow manufactured a new foundation to their lives. He had produced kittens, puppies and ponies. He had eaten revolting morsels at dolls' picnics and stood bareheaded in the rain at the funerals of pet bantams. He had handed handkerchiefs tactfully to the tearful, laughed at bad school reports, rescued them from Nan's rages. Through all their violent and inconsolable griefs he had seemed a rock, and now the rock was crumbling. Aunt Clara was drunk; Nan's only conversation was vague innuendoes uttered in a frightened whisper; Codding and the other men stopped talking whenever they drew near. There was no help from outside and even to each other they could hardly voice their thoughts. Long and desperate silences fell between them.

After Hollis had departed neither spoke for a long time. At last Deb announced in a voice which broke: 'I shall kill myself if they hang Uncle Mark.'

'Don't be silly,' said her brother with a conviction he did not feel, forced by his two years' seniority to offer comfort. 'Of course they won't hang him. He didn't kill Guy Vickers.'

'Then why does he keep drinking?' demanded Deb. 'He'll have to go into a home next.'

'Oh, I expect he's just fed up,' said Jon. It's enough to make anyone drink, having the place lousy with detectives.'

When Hollis reported to him Superintendent Fox agreed that his information was worthy of a conference with the Chief Constable, though he pointed out that there was no hope at present of making an arrest.

'You've no proof,' he told his subordinate as he picked up the telephone, 'and you've got to have the devil of a lot of proof nowadays. You won't get a committal on a murder charge on what you've got. Find the tin of arsenic. Get Mrs. Broughton sober—she may have something to say. See the other guests again and find out whether Broughton was seen anywhere near the mantelpiece—Lincombe 200,' he interrupted himself to tell the operator.

Hollis said, 'I've got Broughton rattled. If I keep on at him he'll give something away. He's drinking hard; he'll break before long.'

'I don't know about that,' said Fox. 'Tough lot, these hunting people. They—' He broke off as the Chief Constable came on the line. 'Coming over,' he remarked, replacing the receiver. 'Come on, just time for a cup of tea.'

Hollis retold his case against Mark Broughton to the Chief Constable. 'And now I've got him properly rattled,' he finished with pride. 'He's drinking a lot too much, and this afternoon he told me to get out of his house and said he wouldn't answer any more questions except in the presence of his solicitor.'

'Tch, tch,' said the Chief Constable. 'Pity we've reached that stage so early. Except for the old nurse's story we've very little to go on, very little. It's all so circumstantial, but of course you realize that. And then this hunt quarrel is really rather a trivial matter. I don't think that in itself it's much of a motive unless there's something more behind it. One would have to be very unbalanced to

56

murder for that sort of thing and, so far, we've no evidence that he is unbalanced.'

'I understand the hunt means a great deal to Mr. Broughton, sir,' Hollis said. 'Commander Chadwick's words were that "he *lived* for the pack". And then, on the old nurse's showing we could easily establish that he's a violent and quarrelsome type of man.'

'Hmm. You're taking it he's a fanatic?'

'Quite, sir. It won't be difficult to produce evidence of that. The difficulty's going to be to prove he introduced the poison into Vickers' glass. None of the others present at the party are willing to admit that he even approached Mr. Vickers. In fact they're being very evasive—I shouldn't have thought that people of their social standing would have wished to assist a criminal, but I gather that a Master of Foxhounds is something of a local king.'

'Well, well,' said the Chief Constable, and he hummed a few bars before he spoke again.

'You know, I still think we ought to call in the Yard, Fox,' he said. 'I realize you're against it; but we haven't the experience they have, we can't expect to have it and there's no disgrace attached to asking for specialized help in a case of this kind—in fact it's rather the other way about. If the Press start clamouring or old Vickers button-holes his M.P. we shall be on the mat for not realizing our limitations.'

'Call in Scotland Yard, sir?' said Hollis speaking out of turn. 'Call in the Yard with a case three parts solved? You'll be handing it to them on a plate.'

Fox scratched his nose. 'Well, it's for you to say, sir, but

—' The telephone rang and with a sigh of exasperation he broke off and lifted the receiver.

'Dr. Skindle, sir,' said the cadet on the switchboard. 'I told him that you were in conference, but he says that it's of the utmost urgency.'

'Put him through,' said Fox.

Dr. Skindle spoke loudly and clearly; all three of them could hear him. 'Fox?' he said. 'Skindle here. Look, I'm at the kennels at Lapworth. Mrs. Broughton's in a bad way. She's not going to last long and, unless I'm a Dutchman, it's arsenic again.'

CHAPTER SEVEN

IT WAS Tuesday morning when the Assistant Commissioner sent for Detective Chief Inspector James Flecker. The A.C. was a dark, dyspeptic man of immense capability. He worked endlessly and at speed and expected those under him to do the same. Given to sarcasm, he suffered fools not at all and was much feared in Central Office.

'Just the thing for you, Flecker,' he said. ' "Death Stalks Rural England. Arsenic in the Stirrup Cup. Master of Foxhounds goes Berserk", or so the local constabulary appear to think. Here you are, get down to Melborough as fast as you can and straighten them out. And for Christ's sake buck up about it, because with Linden sick and Canning on holiday I'll be sending myself out on the next job.'

' "Chief Inspector Solves Killing at Supersonic Speed," ' said Flecker, taking the proffered folder. 'Right, sir,' and he turned to leave the room.

'You'd better take Browning,' the A.C. called after him. 'Tell Sutton I don't care what he's on, you've got to have him.'

'Thank you, sir.'

'You needn't sound so grateful,' said his superior. 'I only do it for my own peace of mind.'

Sergeant Browning was delighted. 'That *will* make a nice change, sir,' he said. 'It's some time since we had an outing together. I'll just dash home and pack a bag.'

59

'I'll call for you then,' said Flecker. 'It's on the way.'

Then he went back to his rooms at the top of a gloomy house in an unfashionable quarter of Kensington, packed a modest bag, had a word with his landlord's wife, left a note for the milkman and was on his way with an alacrity which would have commended itself to the Assistant Commissioner.

Browning's luggage was far less modest. Flecker looked at it with distaste. Good God! How long do you think this is going to take us—six months?'

'Just as well to be prepared, sir. I dare say we shall be moving in smart circles.'

'Now then,' said Flecker. 'Remember you're a married man and a copper. There's no more room in the boot so you'll have to put that great trunk in the back.'

Free of Outer London, its neighbouring light industries and their attendant housing estates, Flecker told his companion to read the case notes aloud.

'Looks bad for the M.F.H.,' said Browning, when he had finished. 'He sounds a bit of a tartar. They mostly are a bit peppery, these M.F.H.'s. Got to be, I suppose; I wonder if they're chosen because they're like that or if they get like it afterwards?'

'Cause and effect, the eternal mystery,' said Flecker unhelpfully.

'When I was a boy,' Browning went on, 'old Colonel Darcy Blake had the Houghton hounds. He *could* give you a mouthful too. Many's the time I've had the warm side of his tongue. Of course, I was a bit of a lad; always wanted to be up in front; rode the old pony nearly to death. I wanted to go in to hunt service, but father wouldn't hear of it and now look at me—a ruddy policeman.'

'Never mind, your misspent youth is going to stand you in good stead. You can reminisce by the hour with the hunt staff—there's nothing like gossip.'

'Good as a holiday, this is going to be. Only wish it was summertime.'

By the time they stopped for lunch Melborough had begun to appear on the signposts and the countryside had become undulating with hedges dividing the dipping fields. ' "O pastoral heart of England" ', said Flecker, and Browning, assuming professional tones, remarked that it was a nice bit of hunting country.

Melborough took them by surprise. An apparently interminable suburb culminated abruptly in the main street, a wide, tree-lined, vista of ancient houses built in glowing stone. Flecker stopped to ask the whereabouts of County Police Headquarters and was directed to a between-the-wars building in a paler version of the golden stone just beyond the town centre. Leaving the car in the gravelled courtyard they walked towards the station.

Browning looked his chief over. 'Your coat belt's twisted, sir, and your tie's a bit round to the right.'

'Oh, hell!' said Flecker; but he obediently straightened his tie and untwisted his belt. Then Browning handed him the folder containing the case notes. 'You'd better have this too,' he said, offering a pencil, 'because, if I remember rightly, yours are always chewed to bits.'

'Thanks ,' said Flecker meekly and led the way in.

As they came into his office Superintendent Fox looked from one to the other and thought, as people always did, that the tall, broad-shouldered, well-dressed man with the greying hair and the Anthony Eden moustache must be Flecker; but Browning, who had been mistaken for the Chief Inspector before, drew back hastily and the Superintendent found himself shaking hands with a younger and far less striking individual. Stocky—he was barely tall enough for police regulations—he had a rather square face above which his dark hair grew in untidy profusion. His wide and shapeless mouth was amiable and it was only his eyes that betrayed his intelligence: dark blue eyes that burned in the slow, good-natured face.

'Pleased to meet you,' said Fox, looking at his watch. 'The Chief Constable should be here in about five minutes.'

When the Brigadier arrived they went through the notes of the case again, after which Fox brought them up to date with a resume of the latest information.

'Broughton's drinking fairly heavily,' he said. 'But he seems able to stand it. We've got two men on him, night and day, but so far he hasn't gone further than the kennels. He gave us permission to search and we've been through the house with a small toothcomb. The results were entirely negative.

'Mrs. Broughton actually died of heart failure caused by the arsenic poisoning. Apparently her heart had been groggy for some time—years on the bottle, I suppose and it wouldn't have taken much to finish her off. She took the stuff in two or three large nips of gin, and the analyst's report indicates that it was a pretty strong solution. There were no fingerprints on the bottle except the deceased's, but there are indications that, previous to her handling, it had been wiped clean. We've contacted the distillers and asked them to trace the sale as quickly as possible.

'The Vickers, inquest was opened and adjourned this morning. Mrs. Broughton's is to be held here on Thursday.'

Flecker was making notes. Browning sighed as he saw an old envelope and the tattered stump of a pencil come into use, and observed with some annoyance that the Chief Constable and Fox had also remarked this unbusinesslike behaviour. You don't do yourself any good, he thought; you'd get yourself promoted twice as fast if you behaved like everybody else.

'Where did Mrs. Broughton usually acquire her liquor?' asked Flecker, stuffing the first envelope into his overcoat pocket and producing another one.

'Mr. Broughton told us that he has a standing monthly order with Baines and Bateworthy, here in Melborough. But lately Mrs. Broughton's consumption had gone up and he said she'd obviously been drinking far in excess of what he provided. He said that he hadn't an idea where she obtained it; but she had a certain amount of money of her own and a separate banking account, so it would be quite easy for her to arrange another supply. The old nurse was too distraught to tell us much, but apparently she didn't know where it came from either—though she was quite certain that there *was* another source of supply.'

'Have you sent the bottle of gin to our lab?'

'No, having established the nature and strength of the poison . . .' began Fox, but the Chief Constable interrupted him.

'We'll soon send it up to the Metropolitan Police if you'd like us to,' he said.

'Thanks,' said Flecker. 'They may be able to give us a lead on what commercial preparation was used. And the P.M. report isn't very detailed,' he went on. 'I don't know how experienced the police surgeon and this Dr. Skindle are, but I think on the whole we'd be wise to get an expert to have a look. I think we should ask them to send Anstruther down, sir,' he said, looking the Chief Constable firmly in the eye.

'Very well,' said Lampton.

Flecker got up. 'If you've got two men looking after the M.F.H. and he's happy with his bottle I'll leave him in the moment and take a look round some of the others first. Oh, by the way, sir,' he asked, turning to Fox, 'can you lend us a large-scale map?'

Fox left the office to fetch one and the Chief Constable turned to the question of where they were going to stay. 'The Coach and Horses is expensive and always full,' he said. 'But they tell me the Station Hotel's reasonable and not too bad.' He looked at Flecker, but the Chief Inspector was lost in thought and had not heard a word.

Browning cleared his throat and when that failed to rouse Flecker, muttered, 'the Chief Constable's asking where we are staying, sir.'

'Staying?' said Flecker. 'Oh, at a pub somewhere, I suppose. I'm a great believer in gossip, sir, and Browning's a genius at making bosom friends of chance acquaintances. Is there a pub in Hazebrook or Lapworth?'

'Not that I know of,' said the Chief Constable. Fox, who had returned with the map, said, 'Try the Dog and Duck at Lollington. They might take you—so many of them don't put people up any more.'

When the two strangers had gone Fox looked at Lampton. 'Dreamy sort of individual sir,' he remarked tentatively.

'Hmm. I can't say I was much impressed. The sergeant looked the better man. Still, it's out of our hands. We can't do more than call them in. I shan't sleep any the worse tonight for knowing we don't carry the can.'

Hecker said, 'You drive,' and he studied his envelopes while Browning made a great to-do of putting back the driving seat and adjusting the mirror. 'Now where do we want to go, sir?' he asked when he had the engine running, for it was obvious that his companion's thoughts were far away.

'Oh, the Chadwicks'. Orchard Cottage, Hazebrook, isn't it?' Flecker searched round for the folder.

CHAPTER EIGHT

'NOW I CALL THAT a pretty place,' said Browning as he drew up in front of the pink-washed cottage 'I bet it's a real picture in summer when the flowers are out. Just the sort of place I'd like to retire to—but there's not a ruddy hope on a police pension.'

'Not a hope,' agreed Flecker. 'Desirable old-world cottages are worth their weight in gold. You'd buy a forty-bedroomed mansion with a park cheaper than a place like this. Look, I don't think this is going to need two of us. I think it would be much better if you drove on to Lollington and found out if the pub will put us up. If I finish here before you're back, I can always go and look round the church.'

'You don't want to hang about looking at churches in this weather,' objected Browning. 'And I'll hang on a minute to see if anyone's at home,' he added, as Flecker left the car. He waited until he saw the cottage door open and Flecker disappear inside and then he drove towards Lollington.

'My husband's out,' Elizabeth Chadwick told Flecker. 'Some sort of governors' meeting, I think. And Hilary's riding—but if I can be of any use?'

'Oh yes,' said Flecker. 'I'm sure you can,' and he followed her into the drawing-room. Today, the log fire burned fiercely and a card table had been set up in front of it on which Elizabeth had evidently been typing. Flecker shed his gloves into the first chair he came to and then turned to inspect the bookcase which took up almost the whole of one wall.

'Is this a cross-section of the family reading matter?' he asked. 'Or an indication of catholic taste?'

'A bit of both,' answered Elizabeth. 'The naval history is read exclusively by my husband and the very learned looking volumes in the bottom shelf are a legacy from my father. I didn't know Scotland Yard was bookish.'

Flecker said, 'Oh dear, I'm off the point. Is this the room where you had the party?'

'Yes, it hasn't felt quite the same since. One can't help remembering that Guy stood there, that someone was watching him, contemplating murder. One waits for Banquo. I *did* hope that it would turn out to be the ceiling at Catton Hall, but now, with Clara dead too, I suppose it *must* be murder.'

'The ceiling?' asked Flecker. 'Oh, you are thinking of Clare Boothe Luce.'

'Yes, that's right.'

'You've known Mr. and Mrs. Broughton for quite a long time, haven't you?' asked Flecker.

Elizabeth pulled ineffectively at the card table. 'Yes, for ten or eleven years, I think. Look, do sit down.' Flecker moved the table for her and took off his overcoat. 'Yes, I think it must be eleven years since Mark called on us and said that he was taking over the hounds,' she went on musingly. 'He was a sweetie and,' she added, 'still is.'

Flecker laughed.

'That stupid Hollis was enough to drive us all mad,' said Elizabeth. 'I suppose Mark swore at him—I nearly did

67

myself.'

'I've never met this Inspector Hollis, so I can't really advance an opinion.' Flecker's voice was casually amiable. 'However, you've got to remember that the poor wretched detective has to sum Mr. Broughton up in half an hour, whereas you've had eleven years to form your opinion. Have you known the Broughtons intimately for all those eleven years?'

'Yes. They're younger than we are—Mark—Mr. Broughton—is forty-one, I think, and his wife was about two years younger—but it never seemed to matter. He always got on very well with my husband and she was a dear, very gay and amusing except when she was in one of her black moods; but they never lasted long. We used to see a great deal of each other.'

'But lately, since things have gone wrong, you haven't seen so much of them?'

'That sounds like a reproach,' said Elizabeth. 'We haven't deserted them. It's just that when people are very proud, and both Clara and Mark are proud, they hate to display their sufferings. They withdraw even from their best friends because they can no longer put on the brave face they feel they should present to the world. It's absurd,' she added vehemently; 'what are friends for but to help in times like these? If one can't help, one can offer comfort; but Mark retreats, throwing up earthworks like a mole, if one says a word. It's the idiotic educational system that does it: they stuff these wretched boys with a lot of half-baked ideas. They force them willy-nilly into the same mould, they turn them out all to a pattern, outwardly conforming, outwardly correct, and underneath they're crawling with inhibitions—tied by a suppressed instinct at every turn.'

Flecker said, 'No comment, I went to a grammar school. . . . I suppose you haven't any idea why Mrs. Broughton started to drink?'

'That's always been a mystery to everyone. Locally she's supposed to have started when a small child fell in the river at Langley. Clara went in after her, which was quite brave, because she's not—wasn't I mean—much of a swimmer, and though the river isn't very wide there it flows fairly fast. By the time she got the child out with the help of some of the villagers who'd arrived, it was too late. Clara went absolutely frantic, she seemed convinced the whole thing was her fault, and no one could persuade her that she'd done everything that could have been done; not even the Coroner. She took to drink with a vengeance about then, but Mark said that the child wasn't the cause, it was the last straw. He said Clara had been drinking a good deal on the quiet for some time. Once, when he was in a confidential mood, he told me that everything would have been all right if they'd had children. He said Clara hadn't wanted them at first and then, when she did want them, they failed to materialize. Of course he's devoted to his orphan nephew and niece, but they arrived on the scene too late to help Clara.'

'You make him sound a very unlikely murderer,' said Flecker. 'But circumstances can make the nicest people desperate. He may have suddenly seen his wife as the sodden drunk she was, or he may have fallen in love with

69

someone else and realized what he was missing.'

'Oh no,' Elizabeth answered quickly. 'Mark hadn't done that, I'm sure he hadn't. I heard him talking to Clara at our party; they were leaving their coats in the dining-room and he didn't know anyone was listening. He was talking to her in the sweetest possible way; telling her she was only to have one drink. Except when he's hunting hounds, Mark's the most patient of men . . . There's Hilary,' she went on as a door slammed in the brief silence which followed. 'Would you like some tea? I can put the kettle on while you talk to her.'

'I'd love some,' answered Flecker, looking wistfully round the firelit room. 'But I think my poor sergeant is back waiting patiently outside. I'll just have a word with Miss Chadwick and then I really must go. You've been a great help to me. You've balanced my colleague's case against Mr. Broughton by being equally biased in the opposite direction.'

Elizabeth laughed, for Flecker had spoken lightly. Then she said, 'This is my daughter. Hilary, this is Chief, I mean Detective Chief Inspector Flecker of Scotland Yard.'

Hilary shook Flecker by the hand and he saw that she had her mother's enormous eyes, but they were blue instead of brown. She had, too, the same beautiful complexion. Her yellow hair was windswept and hung in tendrils on her shoulders. 'To sport with Amaryllis in the shade,' thought Flecker. 'I'm leaving,' he said, 'but I thought I might ask you something on the way out. You knew Mr. Vickers well; had he ever said anything to you about this hunt quarrel?'

'Yes, we discussed it quite a bit. I don't know that can remember his exact words—everything has begun to seem a very long time ago. Let's go back to the fire, I'm frozen and this is going to take ages. When Guy first told me that he'd spoken to Colonel Clinkerton, I told him that his suggestion wouldn't go down at all well; but I couldn't make him see that poor hunts as well as poor people have their pride. Then he said that he'd only spoken to Clinkerton in confidence and that if the suggestion *was* unsuitable he would keep it to himself. I told him that Colonel Clinkerton had never kept anything to himself in his life, that the whole hunt would know in two minutes and that Mark would be furious.' She stopped abruptly and considered the word. 'I said furious,' she repeated looking at Flecker, 'but I didn't mean the sort of fury that would lead to violence, or anything of that sort.'

'You meant that he would be exceedingly annoyed?' suggested Flecker.

'Yes,' Hilary looked pleased. 'That's exactly what I meant. One uses these words— a person has only to look a bit disagreeable and everyone rushes round saying he's *livid.*'

'Habitual exaggeration,' said Flecker. 'I wonder what makes us do it. Go on.'

'Well, Guy said that he didn't care two pins or words to that effect. He said he wasn't afraid of Mark or anyone else. He said that if a business was on the rocks it was only too glad to collect a sleeping partner with a bit of cash and that he was prepared to be lavish. He said also that he didn't want to hunt hounds or run the kennels and finally,

71

when he was tired of arguing with me, he said that if the committee didn't like his suggestion they could ignore it, and that he'd write to the Scarford Vale who were advertising for a joint master in *Horse and Hound*.'

'And the committee did ignore it?' asked Flecker.

'Well, actually they haven't met; but of course Colonel Clinkerton told everybody so there was a terrific buzz among the subscribers and the farmers and everyone else. The people who hunt to jump were mad to have Guy, but the farmers and the people who are really keen on the hunt would never go against Mark.'

'This excitement didn't stop your parents from inviting both of them to the same party?'

'No. Well, actually the invitations had gone out earlier but we thought it rather a silly quarrel; we thought it was time it was made up. My father did just mention to Mark that Guy would be there and he didn't protest too violently so we left it at that.'

'And at the party?' asked Flecker.

'Oh, they just glared at each other from opposite ends of the room. I talked to them each in turn.'

'From my colleague's notes I gather that there was a moment when you were not talking to either of them.'

'Yes, that's right. I was going back to talk to Guy but he was talking to Colonel Holmes-Waterford, so I couldn't.'

'If I'd been doing the evil deed, I wouldn't have done it while you were talking to Vickers,' said Flecker thoughtfully. 'I'd have nipped in while Mrs. Broughton was with him, hoping that in her fuddled state she'd be less likely to notice.'

'I can't see how anyone did it,' objected Hilary. 'I'm sure Guy kept hold of his glass.'

'Somebody did do it though,' said Flecker. 'And the same somebody murdered Mrs. Broughton and may take it into his head to kill again.'

Hilary paled a little at his earnestness and then she said, 'Supposing we had a bottle of gin that had somehow got contaminated with arsenic and supposing Clara pinched it at the party—they say that alcoholics lose their principles and will do anything for a drink.'

'Unfortunately your father mixed the cocktails in the kitchen. He used, if I remember rightly, only one bottle of gin and everyone who drank cocktails was served from the same shaker. Practically everyone did drink cocktails and those who didn't had either sherry or a whisky. In fact if it had been your gin three-quarters of your guests would have been dead and not just Vickers.'

Hilary said, 'There *must* be some explanation—'

Flecker smiled. 'Don't worry,' he said. 'We only started this afternoon, time will show.'

'No good you making excuses, sir,' said Browning, when Flecker hurried out to the car. 'I saw her. A real smasher. I'm surprised to see you out now; you wouldn't have seen me for a fortnight.'

'Work and play don't mix,' said Flecker primly. 'Captain Bewley also lives in Hazebrook; I think we'd better save the ratepayers' petrol and see him while we're here.'

'New Farm,' said Browning. 'I've been reading those notes through till I nearly know them by heart.'

Bob Bewley, a wiry little man in cavalry twill trousers,

a leather patched hacking jacket and a cap, was filling wooden water buckets in his stableyard.

'Oh, so they've called you in, have they?' he said when Flecker explained that they were from Scotland Yard. 'I didn't think that other chap had much in his top storey. I'll just give these brutes their buckets and then we'll go inside.'

Browning was inspecting the horses over the loose-box doors. 'A very nice stamp of hunter, sir,' he said to Bewley.

Bewley grinned. 'Can't sell you one, can I, Sergeant?' he asked. 'They're all quiet with hounds, guaranteed good jumpers and warranted sound.'

'I'll be back to see you when my pools come up,' said Browning. 'I've had nineteen two weeks running.'

Bewley turned out the lights. 'Come on,' he said. 'Let's get inside and have a drink. What with my prospective purchaser bumped off, my day's hunting cancelled and poor Clara no more, the bottle is all that's left me.'

'Did you know Mrs. Broughton well, sir?' asked Flecker as he followed him into the kitchen.

Bewley poked at the range. 'Would you rather be uncomfortable in here or cold and uncomfortable in the parlour?'

'Just uncomfortable,' answered Flecker.

'Mother's ruin?' Bewley brandished a bottle. Flecker shook his head. 'Sorry, we're on duty,' he said. Browning looked at the range. 'The kettle's singing,' he remarked. 'Now a nice cup of tea . . .'

'Right you are,' said Bewley obligingly and he turned to

the cupboard.

'I'll make it, sir,' offered Browning. 'While you answer the Chief Inspector's questions.'

'That's why policemen go about in pairs; I've always wondered. There's the teapot; here's the tea. Fire ahead, *Chief* Inspector.'

'Did you know Mrs. Broughton well?' Flecker asked again.

'Yes, and you needn't looked surprised. I wasn't always as seedy as I am now. When I first came here I was young and hopeful. I still had my war service gratuity, my demob suit and my first wife, I think. Yes, that's right, my marital relations were excellent. Mark had just become master and I soon found him a couple of horses; good ones too, never sell a bad 'un in your own hunt, that's my motto.'

'Where do you keep the milk, sir?' asked Browning.

'Oh, in the cupboard. My wife went back to mother and she took the fridge with her—my second wife, that is.'

Flecker asked, 'Why should anyone murder Mrs. Broughton?'

'It's beyond me,' Bewley answered. 'Why should anyone murder Vickers for that matter? I think there's someone about with a screw loose.'

'You arrived early at the Chadwick party, before Vickers. You didn't see anything at all unusual going on with the drinks?'

'No, I didn't. You're not going to suggest that Chadwick poisoned him, are you?' he asked indignantly.

'Sugar, sir?' said Browning. 'One or two?'

'Two for me,' answered Bewley, looking inquiringly at Flecker.

'The Chief Inspector doesn't take it, sir,' Browning told him. 'Ah, I've been longing for a nice cup all afternoon,' he added, sipping in a satisfied manner.

Flecker pushed back a lock of unruly hair, looked at Bewley and said, 'It's no use being indignant. Someone at that party killed Vickers and the same person, almost certainly, killed Mrs. Broughton. Of course it's not pleasant to think that you've been hunting and drinking with a murderer, but there's no sense in burying your heads in the sand. Mrs. Chadwick thinks it must be chronic arsenic poisoning caused by a painted ceiling at Catton Hall; Miss Chadwick favours a contaminated gin bottle; you want a madman. All right, have your madman, but face the facts—he's one of your friends.'

'O.K., Chief Inspector, you win,' said Bewley meekly. 'I arrived first. I talked to the Chadwicks, who appeared to be their normal selves, with all screws at the appropriate tension. They don't altogether approve of me, but they're always very nice and polite and Hilary's glad of the odd horse to hunt, especially when her brother's home on leave. When Vickers and Antonia Brockenhurst arrived Vickers monopolized Hilary; Charlie poured out drinks; everyone seemed to be having the cocktail—it was one of Charlie's specials. Couldn't pin the murders on Antonia, could you?' he asked suddenly. 'She'd be no loss.'

'I'll do my best for you,' said Flecker with a grin. 'Go on.'

'Well, the Chadwicks, Ma and Pa, and I, had to talk to

Antonia. She rides a bloody good race, I'll give her that, but she's hell indoors. We all wagged our tails like mad when Holmes-Waterford and then the Dentons came in.' He dwelt for a moment on the Dentons' name and then went on. 'The party got going after that and I'm afraid I got a bit high on Charlie's special. I remember that I collected Clara from Vickers, who was looking at her as though she were something the cat had brought in, and that we had a nice chat in a corner until Mark came to take her home. The next excitement was Vickers feeling sick. I was roaring with laughter at the great man passing out on a couple of short drinks but luckily, Charlie, Elizabeth and Steve Denton were sober enough to realize that it wasn't that. When they reached the stage of sending for Skindle and then the ambulance, I sobered up sharpish.'

'Did everyone behave more or less as you would have expected them to behave?' asked Flecker. 'You didn't see any unexpected hysterics?'

'No, no hysterics, no fireworks, no nothing. We all behaved like—no wait—Antonia Brockenhurst, she went a greenish colour. I thought—Oh God, it's the crab patties, now we'll all be off to hospital. Then Charlie, who was acting as a sort of liaison officer between Elizabeth and Steve, who'd got Guy upstairs, and the rest of us in the drawing-room, came in and said that Skindle was sending Guy to hospital and that he was a very sick man indeed; and Antonia went a shade greener, and later on gave a sort of whimper and said, "why doesn't that ambulance come?" '

'You haven't invented this because Miss Brockenhurst would be "no loss", have you?' asked Flecker.

'No,' Bewley answered emphatically. 'It's the truth and nothing but the truth, so help me God.'

'All right,' said Flecker. 'Now tell me your opinion of Mr. Broughton; I haven't met him yet.'

'Mark wouldn't hurt a fly. He wouldn't kill a kitten, much less Clara.'

'What about foxes?' asked Flecker.

'Well,' Bewley grinned, 'he has to kill a few to please the farmers and keep hounds in blood, otherwise he wouldn't. But seriously Mark's a very good chap. He's the sort of person one trusts with one's money and, though he's so dam' attractive to women, with one's wife. He is also a fool. He thinks that everyone is as trustworthy as he is. We've all been pretty good about his money. I've never sold him a bad horse, or even an expensive horse.'

'But not so good about his wife?' asked Flecker quietly.

'No, not nearly so good about his wife. Clara was quite a girl, and an M.F.H. is a very busy man. Clara was generous, quite the most generous woman I've ever known. She'd give away her horses, her money, her clothes. If she liked you she wouldn't refuse you anything, and I mean *anything*.'

'I see,' said Flecker. 'Well, thank you very much for being so frank.'

'And thank you for the nice cup of tea, sir,' said Browning. Then he looked at Flecker and asked, 'What have you done with your gloves, sir?'

'My gloves?' Flecker looked guiltily round the room.

'They may be in the car, but I've got a feeling I left them at the Chadwicks'.'

'So have I,' said Browning in resigned tones.

'Never mind,' Flecker told him. 'We'll get them tomorrow.'

Realizing that Flecker was thinking, Browning held his peace until he had the engine running. 'The Dog and Duck, sir?' he asked.

'Can you keep going for another half hour on that cup of tea? Langley's only two miles from here and I'd like to see Miss Brockenhurst tonight.'

'Right you are, sir,' said Browning cheerfully. 'But I know your half hours. And we shan't get any overtime for it—and no thanks either, I don't suppose.'

CHAPTER NINE

No ONE ANSWERED the front door at Sleeches Farm and, after banging for some time, Flecker and Browning made their way round to the back of the house where chinks of light from a window seemed to indicate life.

Browning beat upon the back door with his gloved fist and started a chorus of barking, which angry yells of 'Quiet!' from within failed to silence. The door was finally opened by Antonia Brockenhurst. She was wearing a dirty pair of corduroy slacks and three pullovers, which protruded, in clashing layers, at the cuffs and collar.

'From Scotland Yard,' was all that Flecker attempted to shout above the noise of the dogs.

'Stop it, Tiger,' she roared, and then, in the comparative quiet which followed, she said, 'Do come in, I was just cleaning tack.' The kitchen, an unpretentious farmhouse room with a brick floor and unpainted dresser, was full of dogs; boxers and spaniels of all ages and sizes. The dresser and a deal table were covered with saddlery and the wherewithal to clean it; at another table a redheaded woman with spectacles was cutting up dogs' meat. The visibility was reduced by a pall of smoke which filled the room, and the air reeked of cooking offal. The dogs became boisterously welcoming and the barking abated. Browning amused the boxers while Flecker explained the purpose of their visit; the spaniels were intent on the preparation of their dinners.

'Oh yes, of course,' said Antonia Brockenhurst, 'you'd

better come into the other room. Oh, this is my partner, Miss Chiswick-Norton.'

'I can't shake hands 'cos they're all dog dinnery,' cried Miss Chiswick-Norton shrilly and she smiled a confiding and toothy smile at the two detectives. 'Do tell me, did Mr. Broughton do it?' she asked. 'We've been wondering; bothering our little heads. I'm so fed up that I missed all the excitement. Just like me to go away at the wrong moment. Do you suspect Antonia? Whoo hoo!' She laughed shrilly. 'I've always loved thrillers; it is exciting to meet real detectives. Have you found many fingerprints? Will they hang Mr. Broughton, or will he plead guilty but insane?'

'Mrs. Broughton was enough to drive anyone nuts,' Antonia shouted her partner down. 'She drove me nuts in one afternoon; at the puppy show, do you remember?'

'Oh rather, it was too funny if it hadn't been so embarrassing. She'd escaped from the old lady who looked after her; in the end the children came and took her away. I don't think he ought to have kept children and a drunken wife in the same house, do you? He could have put his wife into a home or sent the children away for their holidays.'

'Mrs. Broughton didn't like being in a home,' said Antonia. 'She hated it and everyone knows that Mr. Broughton likes to take the children about with him.'

'I still think it was wrong. Here we are—dinnies! Boxers in the hall, spaniels in the kitchen, puppies in the scullery; the small fry are so *messy*,' she said with a toothy smile at Browning. Antonia went to the hall and began to shout, 'Tiger, come here, will you! Trixie, Tessa, Tantivy, do as you're told!'

In the kitchen, Miss Chiswick-Norton shrieked, 'Susan, Simon, Sarah—' The dogs rushed obstinately in the wrong directions and the detectives looked at each other in despair.

'Let's get the puppies, sir,' suggested Browning. 'That might help things along a bit.' It was easy enough to collect the puppies, fat squirming spaniel pups and the older boxers, which had reached the lanky stage, and to deposit them in the scullery; the difficulty lay in escaping from the scullery without a puppy accompaniment. In the end Flecker got away by leaving Browning behind. In the kitchen the spaniels were now feeding in an orderly fashion, each wearing a clothes peg to hold back his long ears. 'Look after my sergeant,' Flecker told Miss Chiswick-Norton. 'I'll go through and talk to Miss Brockenhurst.'

The sitting-room was cold with the dampness of a rarely used room and Flecker began to shiver as soon as he sat down.

'This won't take long,' he said. 'First of all, did you see anyone at the Chadwicks' party taking any interest in any glass, full, empty, their own or someone else's? They might have been rescuing a drowning fly, removing cigarette ash or pursuing a piece of cork; I'm interested in the most innocent actions.'

Antonia thought carefully before she answered. 'No, I didn't see anything of that sort at all.'

'You didn't talk to Mr. Vickers, did you?'

'No, only on the doorstep, while we were waiting to be

let in.'

'What did you talk about then?'

'Oh, the weather, I think.'

'And after that?'

'That was all.'

Flecker smiled, 'You must be better at spinning the weather out than I am,' he said. 'I find that it does for one remark, possibly two and then you both say the same thing at the same moment, feel a little foolish and introduce some other topic hastily.'

'We just waited in silence.'

Flecker felt that there was a tension in the air; he decided on a shot in the dark.

'My notes tell me that you're a very well-known point-to-point rider,' he said. 'Did Mr. Vickers ever take part in a point-to-point?'

'Yes, at one time he raced quite a bit, then he broke his collar bone two seasons running and I think his parents made him give it up.'

'How long ago was this?'

'Oh, about five or six years ago, I suppose.'

'Did he come to Catton Hall in those days?'

'No, I don't think so. I don't think the Pierces had it then.'

'Where did you live then, before you came here?'

'Barsetshire,' answered Antonia, avoiding his eye.

You were good-looking once, thought Flecker, before you neglected your face and became hardboiled. You're about the same age as Vickers and they tell us 'Heaven has no rage, like love to hatred turned'. 'Mr. Vickers also came from Barsetshire, I believe,' he said.

'Yes.'

'I expect, that with riding as a common interest, you knew each other?' he suggested gently.

'When we were children we belonged to the same pony club and hunted with the same pack.'

'And then you grew up and went to the same hunt balls?'

'That's old history,' answered Antonia, turning on him suddenly. That's all over and done with. Guy's had plenty of girlfriends. If you want to pry into his love affairs you'd better get a bit more up-to-date; you'll find some much more interesting ones, and you can try in Melborough for a start.'

Flecker said, 'Murder's an ugly thing and the more one casts about for reasons and motives the more old history one stirs up.' He paused. 'Who, was the girl friend in Melborough?'

Antonia was now ashamed of her outburst. 'It's nothing really,' she said. 'I oughtn't to have mentioned it; I was upset.'

'If,' Flecker's voice was emphatic, 'it has the smallest bearing on the case you definitely ought to mention it. This isn't an inquiry into who wrote "Miss Potts is a fool" on the blackboard, this is a matter of life and death—death for two people already. As far as the police are concerned, there's no crime in being lovers, or in committing adultery, and I'm not contemplating a sensational article for the Sunday newspapers on Vickers' love life.'

84

'It was Sonia Denton, the vet's wife, if you must know,' said Antonia. 'Steve Denton went away to help with a foot-and-mouth epidemic last autumn and Guy took Sonia out quite a bit.'

'Are there any more of them?' asked Flecker. 'What about Miss Chadwick?'

'Hilary never cared tuppence for Guy. If she'd married him it would have been for his money; she's been in love with Mark Broughton for years.'

Flecker and Browning were in poor shape when at last they reached the Dog and Duck. Already hungry, cold and tired, they were reduced to an even more dreary state by the sight of their supper.

'I thought it would be best to have it cold,' said Mrs. Gordon, indicating corned beef; beetroot, bread and butter, soft biscuits and soapy cheese, 'Not knowing what time you would be in. Would you like a cup of coffee? I've got the kettle on.'

'Yes, please,' answered Flecker, 'and two double whiskies.' Still in their overcoats they crouched dismally over the tiny electric fire until the whisky began to revive them. Then they tackled the unappetizing meal.

'East, west, home's best,' said Browning suddenly. 'If I had my time over again I wouldn't be so daft as to go into the police. I'd go in for one of these thousand a year stunts, I'd be a docker or a miner. Rolling in money, a forty-eight hour week and the whole country quaking whenever you get out of bed on the wrong side. Honestly, sir, we're mugs, that's what we are. What about you? If you had your time over again would you stop on at college and become a parson?'

'The devil dodgers are worse paid than the police; at least they're worse paid than chief inspectors,' answered Flecker. 'And I daresay I wouldn't have made a very good one.'

'I don't know, you'd have been all right in the pulpit. You're just the one to preach a good sermon.'

'What's the public bar like?' asked Flecker, changing the subject. 'Is there a fire?'

'It seemed a nice old-fashioned sort of place, not so poshed up as this,' Browning told him. 'Shall I go and make a recce?'

'I'll come. I've got to have another drink to take away the taste of that filthy coffee. I begin to feel like an F.B.I. type, downing all this Scotch.'

'You don't need to feel American for that,' objected Browning. 'These hunting people are just as bad. Mrs. Broughton drank, Mr. Broughton begins as soon as she's gone, Captain Bewley thinks nothing of having a couple when he ought to be drinking a nice cup of tea—and goodness only knows what he's put away by bedtime.'

'I wonder what starts them off,' said Flecker.

'Having it handy, I expect. Either that, or a nip here and there for Dutch courage, as they grow older and the fences begin to look a bit big.'

The noisy hilarity of the bar died away when Flecker and Browning went in and only partially revived as they ordered and consumed their drinks.

'Well, I'm going to write up my notes,' Flecker told

Browning when he had finished his whisky and had had a few words with the landlord.

'Good night, sir,' said Browning loudly and with great emphasis on the 'sir'. Flecker knew that he was establishing his position—this is the great man, I'm merely one of you.

He felt depressed as he climbed the steep oak stairs, hideously carpeted in red and green, and his depression increased as he surveyed the little beamed bedroom with its alien suite in imitation walnut, linoleum-covered floor and lace-muffled casement. He switched on the electric fire and scuffled in his suitcase for a writing-pad and pen. Now he must try to make something of what he had learned that afternoon. And then, as he sat before the fire, he realized that it wasn't the cold and the corned beef, the pickles or the soapy cheese that had depressed him. It was the cheerless muddle of the world, 'the still sad music of humanity'; the situations which drove people to murder.

CHAPTER TEN

ON WEDNESDAY MORNING Flecker began work at nine o'clock, when he telephoned the police station. He spoke to Fox, who told him that the gin bottle had proved untraceable; it was a product of the war years, of which the firm no longer possessed records. Having cursed mildly and under his breath, Flecker telephoned Marley and Skinner's office in Melborough and asked for Steve Denton. On learning that Mr. Denton had only just come in he sent a message asking for an appointment at ten-thirty that morning, or at any other time that would be convenient. Mr. Denton would see him at ten-thirty. Flecker put down the receiver and wandered out to the yard, where Browning was already warming up the car.

'Denton's safely at work,' said Flecker, 'so we can go and see his missis. We don't want to upset any apple carts, because if the poor wretch doesn't know of his wife's amours, he hasn't a motive.'

'When are we going to fetch your gloves, that's what I want to know?' asked Browning. 'You'll have chilblains for sure.'

'Oh, I'm all right. But the weather seems to be settling down for a real freeze-up.'

'Yes, they won't get hounds out tomorrow; nor Saturday, if you ask me.'

'Are those the hunting days?' asked Flecker.

'Tuesdays and Saturdays with an occasional bye day on Thursdays. They didn't hunt yesterday because of Mrs.

Broughton, but the master's said they can go out tomorrow instead. Haines, that's the kennel huntsman and first whip, is to hunt hounds.'

'You did some overtime last night in the bar,' said Flecker.

'Yes, and very interesting it was too. Quite brought back old times.'

Sonia Denton was at home, but not very pleased to be caught with no make-up, untidy hair and wearing an old housecoat.

'I'm not really dressed; I was just doing the housework; one's chained to the sink nowadays. If you'll just excuse me a minute—"

'Don't you worry, madam,' Browning said quickly. 'We're both married men.' But, nevertheless, Sonia fled.

She took twenty minutes to dress while Flecker and Browning sat in modern chairs with foam rubber seats, on either side of a fitted electric fire. Browning read the romantic short story in Sonia's weekly magazine; Flecker drew gibbets and faces behind bars in his notebook and thought this prying into private lives was the worst part of police work. What did he care if she and Vickers had been lovers? It was none of his business, but she wouldn't realize that; people always suspected one of judging and condemning.

When she came back, it was apparent that Sonia had performed a complete toilette, even to eyebrows and lashes. She looked well dressed in an expensive tweed skirt, a twin-set and high-heeled shoes.

Flecker grinned as he got to his feet. 'A morale raiser?'

he asked, and when Sonia looked at him blankly, added, 'Some people always confront adversity with their best clothes; like captains who put on full dress uniform to go down with their ships.'

'I think it's important to look your best,' Sonia told him. 'I hate this slovenly slacks and pullover business that goes on in the country; it's not feminine. And I don't see why men should go round looking like tramps either. I won't let my husband keep any awful old clothes, so he can't wear them—not even for washing the car.'

Browning said, 'I'm with you, madam, but the Chief Inspector's more of a Bohemian type, and it would be a dull world if we all thought alike.'

'Bohemian, am I? That's the first I've heard of it,' said Flecker. Still, I've been accused of worse things—"

Then he turned to Sonia and went on in a more serious voice, 'Look, Mrs. Denton, I'm afraid we've simply got to drag your private life into this murder inquiry. I'm sure that you want to help us find Mr. Vickers' murderer, and I can assure you that the police are very discreet and that nothing which isn't absolutely essential to the case will be allowed to leak out. The fact is we've learned that you knew Mr. Vickers very much better than you admitted to my colleague, Inspector Hollis.'

'What do you mean?' Sonia asked, but there was no question in her voice. She was trying to gain time.

'Only that you saw a good deal of Mr. Vickers last autumn when your husband was away. Is that correct? We can check up quite easily,' he added when she remained silent. 'But it's bound to give rise to gossip if we start asking questions all round the district.'

'Yes . . .' she said, 'it's true. But it was only for three weeks. I hadn't seen him since, until the other night.'

'Does your husband know about it?'

Sonia stood twisting a cluster of rings on her finger; when at last she answered her voice was barely audible. 'Yes, Steve knew. The busybodies simply rushed to tell him—He isn't a murderer though,' she went on, her voice rising. 'He wouldn't have killed Guy and he certainly wouldn't have killed Mrs. Broughton. There was only one person who had any reason to kill her, and that was Mark. I wonder he hadn't done it before, tied to that disgusting, drunken old hag year after year.' She began to cry angrily, her pretty little face distorted with venom. 'It was Mark who killed Guy, too, just because he didn't want anyone interfering with his hounds. He lives for those hounds; they're his life. Everyone knows that, but they're not going to tell the police, oh no, they don't want Mark hanged; but they don't care what happens to Steve—'

Browning said, 'Now, now, madam. Don't upset yourself; the Chief Inspector's a long way off hanging anyone.'

And Flecker, who was looking at Sonia with a sort of fascinated revulsion, asked: 'Have you any actual proof when you say that Broughton killed Vickers? We know he had a motive, possibly two motives, but did you see or hear anything to make you feel positive he was the murderer?'

'I didn't see him pouring poison into Guy's glass, if that's what you mean,' answered Sonia, sniffing into a tiny

91

handkerchief. 'But it's obvious, isn't it? I can't see why you have to go round upsetting other people, when it's obvious who did the murders.'

'Obviousness is not always evidence,' said Flecker. 'However, let us go on to the party. Can you remember to whom you talked?'

'Yes, I think so,' said Sonia, delighted to be on safer ground. 'First of all I talked to Mrs. Chadwick; I admired the way she'd done the flowers. Not that she'd done much except stick a few Christmas roses into an old-fashioned silver bowl. I remember she held forth for a long time; she's a great talker, it's no wonder her husband never opens his mouth. When I managed to get away from her I had a little chat with Colonel Holmes-Waterford about the weather and the hunt ball. I'm not at all interested in horses or hunting, you know; it wasn't my sort of party at all. I didn't want to go in the first place, but Steve said it was good for business—that's what men always say when they want to justify themselves for dragging their wives to boring parties.

'Well then,' she went on, 'I had no one to talk to so I went to see what Steve was doing. He was talking to Mrs. Broughton. She looked a terrible old ragbag and you could see that she was drunk; she didn't really know what she was saying. I got Steve away as soon as I could, but he only began talking to that grubby little Bob Bewley, so there I was left again. Commander Chadwick came over to speak to me, but he kept on about Nelson, which wasn't very interesting. Then I asked after Antonia Brockenhurst's horses. That's all you can say to her—

"How are the horses, Antonia?" I ask it at every single cocktail party that I meet her at, and then make off as quick as I can. Later on I had a conversation with Hilary Chadwick; she was asking my advice about shops, where I bought my clothes and so on.

'After the Broughtons had left it became a bit more interesting and we talked about how awful she had looked and how she'd been swaying about all over the place and almost poured a drink over Colonel Holmes-Waterford. And then we discussed whether Mark ought to have brought her and whether it was his fault that she drank, and I quite enjoyed myself until poor Guy was taken ill.'

'Did you drink the cocktail?' asked Flecker, when she had finally stopped speaking.

'Yes.'

'What about your husband?'

'He drank it too; it was he who persuaded me to have it. At first I said I'd rather have sherry. But he said Charlie's specials were quite something, so I gave in and had one.'

'One more question,' said Flecker. 'Did you know that Vickers was going to be at this party?'

'No. I shouldn't have gone if I'd known. You see I didn't want to go anyway, but Steve persuaded me. Wild horses wouldn't have dragged me if I'd known Guy was going; it's so embarrassing having to meet. I suppose the busybodies haven't got round to telling the Chadwicks, or else they were so taken up with trying to catch Guy for Hilary.'

'We heard that Miss Chadwick wasn't as interested as all that,' said Flecker. 'We heard, rightly or wrongly, that

93

her . . . er . . . heart was given elsewhere.'

'Oh,' Sonia looked at him with respect. 'Steve forbade me to mention that. He said that Mark had been a good friend to him and that he wasn't in the habit of hitting men when they were down. Men are so silly about friendship.'

Flecker looked at his watch. 'Well, thank you very much, Mrs. Denton. You've been a great help.'

Browning said, 'Good morning, madam,' and followed his Chief down the narrow staircase to the yard below.

'Miaow, miaow, miaow!' said Flecker as soon as he was in the car.

'She's a pretty little thing, though, sir.'

'That won't last, and her wretched husband'll soon find his rose is all thorns; that dear little pussycat is all claws—sharp ones too. I'm looking forward to meeting the poor misguided man; I've a fellow feeling for him.'

'I dunno, sir. I daresay he's happy enough. She keeps the place nice, she's got what it takes, and I expect she's a good little cook.'

'You don't know anything about it,' said Flecker. 'You're happily married to a sensible woman with an exceptionally nice nature; you've no experience of pretty little things who scratch and bite.'

'Mrs. Browning and I have our ups and downs, but that's only natural. You want to have another try, sir. There's no sense in giving up because a thing doesn't work out the first time.'

Flecker's attention seemed riveted on the suburbs of Melborough, through which they were passing, but at length he said, 'I don't think I make much of a husband; women like something more alert and dashing. They want someone punctual and practical; if not good-looking at least well brushed, and with a fair share of the standard attractions—someone who can be shown off to their friends.'

'Not all women by any means,' said Browning with conviction. 'You've been unlucky, fair enough, but you mustn't tar 'em all with the same brush.'

When they reached the King's Street premises of Marley and Skinner the detectives found Steve Denton waiting in the road.

'It's five minutes to eleven,' he pointed out. 'You did say ten-thirty.'

Flecker apologized hastily.

'It's not that I mind waiting,' Steve told him. 'It's just that there's a devil of a lot of work to get through and people always want vets in a hurry.'

'I'll be as quick as I possibly can,' Flecker promised. 'Is there anywhere where we can talk undisturbed?'

Steve thought for a moment. 'We'll try the X-ray room; the office is out of the question—full of people and I think George is in the dispensary.'

He led the way down a narrow alley way and they caught glimpses of bandaged dogs and caged cats as they followed.

'I'm sorry,' said Steve, 'I can't offer you a seat, we'll have to lean. Cigarette?' The policemen shook their heads and he lit one for himself.

Flecker said: 'We called on Mrs. Denton on the way

here.'

Denton's face hardened and when he spoke he kept his voice level with difficulty. 'Wouldn't it have been easier to have questioned us both at the same time?' he asked.

'Well yes, sir, you're quite right, it *would* have been easier,' said Flecker innocently. 'But unfortunately your working hours seem precisely to coincide with ours, which makes things rather difficult.'

'I see. Well, what can I do for you, Chief Inspector?'

Flecker began with his question on the rescue of drowning flies and errant bits of cork from glasses; but the vet was certain that he had seen nothing of that sort. Then Flecker asked him with whom he had talked.

'With Mrs. Chadwick mostly,' was the answer. 'We had quite a long chat. I talked to Charlie too, but he was busy with the drinks. I had a few words with Mrs. Broughton, who seemed, to put it mildly, a bit hazy. A word with Bob Bewley, a word with the Colonel—that's Holmes-Waterford. Oh, yes and a word, in fact several words with Antonia Brockenhurst; she was trying to get a bit of free advice on her grey horse's suspensory ligament. That's about the lot, I think, except for my wife.'

Flecker had been counting on his fingers. 'You didn't speak to Vickers, then?' he asked.

'Well yes, of course I did; but not until he was taken ill.'

'You didn't speak to Miss Chadwick?'

'No, she was very much engaged.'

'And you didn't speak to Mr. Broughton?'

'No. To tell you the truth, I find the Master a little awe-inspiring. I usually wait to be spoken to.'

'And that night he wasn't in a very forthcoming mood?' suggested Flecker.

'I believe not,' answered Steve shortly.

'Did you expect to meet Vickers at this party?' asked Flecker after a pause.

'No.' Steve's voice was even, but it was obvious that he was on his guard.

Flecker pushed ineffectively at his unruly lock of hair. Look,' he said earnestly, 'we've stirred up a good deal of Vickers' past. Don't think we're out to make trouble or that we've just got nasty minds. Murder's an unpleasant business and it's difficult for anyone who's mixed up in it—however innocently—to escape the unpleasantness. All sorts of things that are better forgotten are apt to get dragged up by the officers doing the investigations; but they don't go any further, unless they are absolutely essential to the case. The police are much more discreet than most people suspect.'

Steve was rather red in the face, but he had himself under control. 'All right,' he said, 'I know what you mean. Vickers took advantage of my absence to seduce my wife, but I didn't murder him. I admit I felt like doing so at the time I learned about it, but the feeling evaporated and now the whole affair's just an unpleasant memory.'

'Did you go to Lapworth at all over the weekend?' asked Flecker.

'No.'

'You weren't asked to visit the kennels on Saturday evening or Sunday morning?'

'No, the nearest I went to Lapworth was Mr. Tring's

place at Rollhurst—Upper Rollhurst Farm, I think they call it.' He looked Flecker firmly in the face and went on, 'I can understand that you should suspect me of murdering Guy Vickers; but why in heavens name should I have poisoned poor Clara Broughton? She's never done me any harm; my only feeling towards her was one of pity intense pity.'

'I'm afraid that anyone who murdered Vickers may have had a motive for murdering Mrs. Broughton,' Flecker told him. 'If I had intended to poison Mr. Vickers by calmly adding a solution of arsenic to his cocktail I should have accepted Mrs. Broughton as offering less risk than any of the other guests, and I should have seized my opportunity when I saw her talking to Vickers.'

'Oh,' said Steve thoughtfully, 'I get you there. You mean Clara Broughton was used as a stalking horse but saw what was going on; she turned out not to be quite as scatty as the murderer hoped. Somehow the murderer found out that she knew so he drove over to Lapworth and gave her a nip of arsenic to keep her quiet. Well, I'm sorry, but I can't produce an alibi for the whole of the weekend—sometimes I have a lad from the veterinary college to take round with me in the vac, but the current one is in bed with 'flu. Still, I can provide you with a list of the clients I visited if you like.'

'Don't worry about that at the moment,' Flecker said amiably. 'I won't keep you any longer but I should like a word with your dispenser if he's available—just a routine check-up,' he added apologetically.

'The kennels next, sir?' asked Browning as they climbed into the car.

'I suppose so,' said Flecker with obvious reluctance. 'We've still got Holmes-Waterford to see.'

Browning looked at him critically. You don't seem to fancy meeting Mr. Broughton,' he said.

Flecker looked a little shamefaced. 'You're quite right, I hate meeting murderers; always find myself looking at their necks. Broughton'll be my fourth. There was Langdale, who knifed a coloured boy; I was a sergeant then, working with Canning. There was the celebrated Ma Brown who poisoned her husband and father-in-law and tried to collect the insurance money. And then our mutual friend Carter. They all swung.'

'It's not a bit of good you getting morbid,' the Sergeant said firmly. 'They all deserved to swing; real bad lots they were, every one of them.'

'Yes I know. But is the fourth going to be a bad lot or is he going to turn out to be a much misused man?'

CHAPTER ELEVEN

HOMELY AND WHITEWASHED, with green-painted window frames and doors, the Master's house, adjoining the kennels at Lapworth, seemed to invite sunshine. But, when the detectives drove up it looked forlorn among the bleak grey fields, and the only signs of life were another police car, parked discreetly in the lane and a slow spiral of smoke from a chimney.

Nan kept them a long time on the doorstep before she deigned to answer their knock and when she came her step was slower than before and her face blotchy from weeping. Flecker asked for Mr. Broughton.

''E's in the office,' said Nan. 'I don't know whether 'e'll see you or not. 'E told the last detective to get out. I'm not going in to 'im. There you are, that's the door.'

'Thank you,' said Flecker. He knocked and a voice called 'Come in,' in weary tones. Mark Broughton was writing letters at a flat-topped kneehole desk. He looked tired and his eyes were bloodshot, but to Flecker he seemed sober enough.

'We're from Scotland Yard,' said Flecker. 'I'm Chief Inspector Flecker and this is Sergeant Browning.' He paused and added in his meekest tones: 'And we'd be glad of your help.'

Mark looked at him quizzically. 'That's a new line,' he said.

'It's a new policeman,' Flecker replied.

'Well?' Mark asked warily.

Flecker said, 'Sergeant Browning is very interested in horses and hounds; he used to hunt as a boy. Might he go and look round outside?'

Suddenly Mark smiled and Flecker realized how great his charm must be when he was untroubled by adversity. 'Certainly,' he answered. 'Ask for Haines or Philips and say I sent you.'

'Thank you, sir,' said Browning, looking doubtfully at Flecker. 'I used to hunt with the Houghton when old Colonel Darcy Blake was master. Many's the good day I've had with him, on the old pony.'

'Haines was second whip to the Darlington Woodland at some point in his career. Aren't they an adjacent hunt to the Houghton?' asked Mark.

'That's right, sir. I've had the odd run into their country. Great one for digging, the old Colonel was and he used to swear blue murder when they went to ground in the Darlington country; it was a fairly frequent occurrence too, with all the big woodlands they've got there.'

'Go and look round before the men go to lunch,' said Flecker.

'Sure you don't want me, sir?' asked Browning. 'I dare say there'll be plenty of other opportunities for me to look round.'

'*Quite* sure,' Flecker told him. Reluctantly, Browning left the office and, as the door shut behind him, Mark said, 'I think your sporting sergeant is afraid that you'll be my next victim.'

Flecker laughed. 'No, it's not that; he doesn't think my

101

method of taking notes is efficient and he's always expecting me to make some irreparable police *faux pas*. He's not exactly critical, it's just that he wants to save me from myself.'

'Well, what do you want of me?' asked Mark.

'Answers to a multitude of questions, I'm afraid,' Flecker told him.

'I've already told one policeman that I won't answer any more questions except in the presence of my solicitor,' said Mark.

Flecker looked him in the face. 'If you're guilty of murder that is the most sensible thing you can do,' he said. 'On the other hand if you're innocent it's an absurd line to take.'

'Your predecessor told me I was guilty,' said Mark contentiously.

'My predecessor was a fool,' countered Flecker, his voice brusque and sharp. The two men glared at each other over the desk and then suddenly Mark gave way.

'Oh, go on then,' he said. 'Ask. After all I needn't answer if I don't want to.'

'First question, may I sit down, sir?'

'Of course,' Mark answered. 'Sorry, what little social sense I had seems to have left me.'

Flecker sat down and produced his notebook, a pile of old envelopes and two equally disreputable pencils. Then he tugged distractedly at his hair and said, 'There are so many things I want to ask you that it's impossible to know where to begin.'

'Why not ask me if I killed Vickers and, or, my wife,'

suggested Mark. He spoke quietly and with extreme bitterness.

Flecker looked up from his notes. 'Well, did you?'

'No.' Mark seemed to search for words to qualify his monosyllable but to be too tired to find them.

'The evidence against you is largely circumstantial,' said Flecker, suddenly becoming businesslike. 'I think it would best serve us to begin at the beginning and go through the whole lot; interrupt me if I go off the rails or if you've anything to add.

'Among the guests at the Chadwicks' party, there were three people who had grievances against Vickers. You were one.'

'It's comforting to learn that I wasn't the only one,' interrupted Mark.

'But,' Flecker went on, 'it is your arsenic that is missing. Can't you throw any light at all on the disappearance of that tin of weedkiller?'

'No.'

Flecker thought he detected a slight reservation in the answer and decided to gamble on it. 'And yet,' he said gently, 'we know that you asked Mrs. Broughton what she'd done with it, and we know that you spent all Saturday night looking for it.'

He waited, apprehensively, for an outburst. Mark got up, pushing his chair back violently, and walking round the desk came and leaned against the chimneypiece. Flecker, realizing what a big man he was, found him uncomfortably close. Mark looked down at him and said, 'You know, I suppose, that my wife drank?'

'Yes.'

'Well, if you had someone in the house who was barely responsible for her actions and something disappeared, what would you think and do?'

'I see. Was she in the habit of roaming about the garden?'

'Yes, she'd give Nan, her old servant, the slip and go out without a coat on the coldest of days. She had a sort of mania for the summerhouse.'

'But why should she have killed Guy Vickers?' asked Flecker.

'I've no idea unless she'd heard me cursing and swearing about him and thought that she would do me a last service as a sort of gesture. She was given to gestures.'

'You say "a last service". Does that mean you believe she committed suicide?' asked Flecker.

'What else can I think? I didn't kill her; Nan and the children wouldn't have killed her; we had no visitors on Saturday or Sunday. And then, when she was dying,' he fiddled with the clock on the chimneypiece as he spoke, 'she kept murmuring "poor Guy." '

'You thought that that was a sign of remorse?'

'I didn't know what else to think,' Mark answered.

'Well, I think we can dismiss that theory entirely,' Flecker said emphatically. 'I don't believe Mrs. Broughton killed Vickers and I'm sure she didn't commit suicide. Would an intending suicide bother to poison a whole bottle of gin? Would she wipe off all the fingerprints of previous handlers? Would she have had an old and now untraceable bottle, presumably filled for the occasion with the poisoned gin?'

'I had no idea of all this,' said Mark. 'But why should anyone murder Clara?'

'I was hoping you might be able to help me with that point,' said Flecker. 'But there is one obvious motive; she saw something she wasn't meant to see at the Chadwick party; wittingly or unwittingly she constituted a danger to Vickers' murderer who, consequently, had to get her out of the way.'

Mark went on playing with the clock in silence. After a pause Flecker asked, 'You didn't find any trace of that tin of arsenic, did you?'

Mark shook his head, 'Not a sign.'

'Nor did the local police,' said Flecker. 'Of course it's possible the old man was mistaken.'

'That's what I thought,' said Mark, until I tried to shake him. He's absolutely certain it was there on Wednesday; he's ready and willing to swear to it.'

There was another silence and Flecker noticed that the unfortunate clock was now standing on its head. At last Mark spoke again. 'If Clara, my wife, had seen anyone poison Vickers she'd have told me,' he said. 'I'm sure she would and, anyway, who could have got in here to poison her? None of it makes sense.'

'Yes, that's rather the trouble so far as we're concerned. You see, it would have been very easy for you to have killed Mrs. Broughton.'

'And why should I suddenly poison my wife?' demanded Mark. 'The situation hadn't changed in any way and I had put up with it for five years.'

'There's always the last straw,' said Flecker.

'And, as far as I can make out, I'm supposed to have murdered Vickers because he wanted to be joint master—of all the bloody silly ideas. Anyway,' he went on, righting the clock and then turning to face Flecker, 'you're sure my wife had nothing to do with it?'

'I'm sure she didn't kill Vickers and then take her own life.'

'Thank you,' said Mark. He yawned and then asked: 'Any more questions?'

'Did you drink the cocktail at the Chadwicks' party?' asked Flecker.

'Good God, no! I can't stand those naval concoctions; you can't hunt hounds with a splitting head, or at least I can't. I drank whisky. Another nail in my coffin?' he asked as an afterthought.

'No, rather the opposite. You would have had to poison Vickers' actual drink. It would have been much easier to have poisoned one's own and then swapped glasses. If anyone noticed, one could pass it off as a genuine mistake.'

'Yes, I see,' said Mark thoughtfully. 'Sorry, I thought it was mine" and then you simply pour the lethal dose among your hostess's Christmas roses and wait until the next party. Whoever did in Vickers had probably had several goes already.'

'Quite likely,' said Flecker. 'It's a good time of year for parties.'

Mark sighed. 'But who out of all those people could possibly have behaved like that? I've known them all for

106

years. I don't believe there's one of 'em capable of it.' He sounded very tired and frustrated.

'If I were you, sir. I'd try and get some sleep,' said Flecker, and he grinned inwardly to hear himself talking like Browning.

'You trying to get me to the slaughterhouse in good condition?' asked Mark.

'No, I just feel that you might be of more use to me if you weren't quite so tired. Would you mind if I went and talked to Miss Hatch?'

'Not in the least.' Mark yawned again. 'But don't expect to hear a good word for me. If Nan had had her way, I should have been summarily dealt with long ago; strung up on the walnut by the gate. I think,' he went on, 'I'll take your advice. Would you tell her I've gone to bed and don't want any lunch?'

'Very good,' said Flecker. 'And thank you very much.'

'What for? Not throwing you out?'

'Precisely,' said Flecker. 'Only, in the police we call it co-operation.'

He found Nan in the kitchen making apple dumplings.

'May I come in and talk to you?' he asked. 'Don't stop your cooking.' He looked at the apples with interest. 'I always wondered how they got inside.'

'The children like them,' said Nan, banging viciously at her pastry. 'That Mrs. Tucker, called herself a cook, but she didn't make them properly. Lard and a nice drop of milk I put in, then there's some goodness in it. There's no goodness in water. It was just the same with 'er soups. Vegetables and a drop of water, where's the goodness in that? Time and time again I said to 'er why ever don't you get some bones and boil up a nice stock?'

'And wouldn't she take your advice?' asked Flecker.

'Not 'er! You might as well have spoken to your little finger. She turned nasty in the end; went and got a job up in London, so she said. They won't think much of 'er cooking up there.'

'And now you have to do it?' said Flecker.

'I works myself to death for Mr. Broughton and those children and not a word of gratitude do I get. I'd 'ave left years ago if it hadn't been for Mrs. Broughton. Forty-two years I've been with 'er family. Thirty years with her ladyship and twelve years with Mrs. Broughton. It was a pity she ever married 'im.'

'But they got on well at first, didn't they?' asked Flecker.

'New brooms,' said Nan, banging the dumplings down in their baking dish, 'always sweeps clean.' She turned to put the dish in the oven and went on, 'It was all right so long as she went riding and hunting with 'im. She'd ride all them big 'orses, and she only a little thing. Used to jump *anything*—anything, didn't matter how 'igh it was, she'd be over; that's what they used to tell me. Lovely she looked in 'er hunting clothes, white stock and all. I used to tie it for her. "Nan," she'd say, "you do it so much better than I do; it never moves when you tie it for me." Then there were all the hunt balls and the parties, very gay they were at first. Of course, she needn't 'ave taken 'im. She had plenty of other admirers; plenty of proposals too. She was such a pretty little thing.' Nan sat down at the floury

108

table and wept bitterly.

What consolation could one offer, Flecker wondered, for the old nurse wasn't weeping for the poor drunken wreck who'd died on Sunday, but for the brave gay figure of long ago. He felt his anger rising against Broughton, who'd spoken so casually. He'd shown no shame at having taken something so vivid and reduced it so low. Marriage didn't always work out; however good your intentions you could fail, he knew that from his own experience. But at least Broughton could have given his wife her freedom.

'What actually drove Mrs. Broughton to drink?' he asked Nan gently.

'She wouldn't tell me. Time and time again I begged 'er to tell me, but she never would and she wouldn't have a word against him, neither. Not a word. I wrote and told 'er ladyship and she came down, but it wasn't a bit of use. She spoke to him about it, but directly 'e started on to Mrs. Broughton she went abroad. Just packed up and went and we didn't see 'er for three months. She wrote to him and said that she wanted to think things out—or that's what 'e told me. When she came back things were better for a time and then she got worse and worse and 'e took to spending all day with them 'ounds. Her ladyship died and there was no one I could send for. I did all I could, but it wasn't a bit of use . . . and she was such a lovely little baby . . .' Tears overwhelmed her again and Flecker stood by, feeling utterly inadequate. Browning always found some consolation to offer, he told himself. But what in honesty could he find to say? It was the loss of a life's work.

'Can't I get you a drink or something?' he asked

diffidently.

'It's not a bit of use you trying to ask me no questions today.' Nan pulled herself together sharply. 'You run along now and come back tomorrow or the next day, when that there inquest's over, and then I'll show you my photographs.'

Flecker, relieved to find she could face the thought of a tomorrow, agreed and thanked her politely for her help.

'Gone one,' said Nan ignoring him and bustling round the kitchen. 'Goodness knows what time we're going to 'ave lunch.'

CHAPTER TWELVE

FLECKER AND BROWNING drove back to the Dog and
Duck for lunch and, as they ate roast beef and Yorkshire
pudding, Flecker tried to sort out his notes while he
listened to Browning.

'Broughton seems well enough liked. Haines said he
wouldn't deny that the master was a "warm one to whip
in to," and Philips, that's the stud groom, said he'd been
like a bear with a sore head since the weedkiller walked,
but otherwise there were no complaints. Codding, the old
gardener, thinks no end of him, but he's still certain that
the weedkiller was on the shelf in the shed on
Wednesday. They've all had strict instructions not to
discuss the murders in front of the children. Those are a
nice couple of kids, sir. Little monkeys, I should think. Up
to all manner of mischief according to what the men were
saying, but good little riders. They were in the saddle
room, getting one of the girl grooms to ask them
questions; something to do with a pony club exam. We
had a good laugh over some of the answers.'

'In fact you had a nice morning,' said Flecker, through a
mouthful of the prunes and custard which had followed
the roast beef. 'While I was trembling in the company of a
volcanic M.F.H. or trying to stem Nan's tears.'

'They don't seem to care much for Nan outside,' said
Browning. 'They reckon she's an old tartar.'

'Well, I reckon she's had something to put up with in

111

her time. I'm not surprised she's turned sour. I'm going to telephone Colonel Holmes-Waterford,' Flecker went on, getting up as he finished his last mouthful. 'We've got to see the Chief Constable at three, or at least, I have, for my sins. I thought we might visit the Colonel on the way there.'

'And there was me hoping to snatch forty winks,' said Browning in resigned tones.

'You're not as afraid of the A.C. as I am,' said Flecker. 'Have you got threepence? I've run out of change.'

At Lapworth Manor the butler took a message and then returned to the telephone to say that the Colonel would see the Chief Inspector at two-fifteen.

Browning joined his chief as he replaced the receiver. 'If we're going to visit all these military gentlemen, we'd better take a clothes brush to you, sir,' he remarked, producing one and advancing on Flecker. 'And isn't this Colonel Holmes-Waterford on the County Council? If I remember rightly he is, so everything said in that quarter will go straight back to the Chief Constable.'

Flecker, who was submitting to being brushed, though not with very good grace, said, 'The bark of military gentlemen is notoriously worse than their bite, and if you think I'm going to put on police college airs for either of them, you're mistaken.'

'What *do* you do with your trousers at night, sir?' asked Browning. 'They look to me as though they spent last night on the floor.'

'Come on,' said Flecker. 'That's quite good enough; if there's one thing your military gentlemen hate, it's to be kept waiting.'

Browning was impressed by Lapworth Manor. 'Quite puts our little pink cottage in the shade, sir, doesn't it? Still, I don't know that I'd want it; it doesn't look very homely to me.'

Gold showed them into the library and there was time for Browning to warm himself at the log fire and for Flecker to inspect the bookshelves before Douglas Holmes-Waterford, with Pluto and Toby at his heels, came in.

'Good afternoon, Chief Inspector,' he said, advancing on Browning, who retreated behind the armchair.

Flecker hastily returned a book to the shelf and came across the room. 'Good afternoon, sir,' he said. 'I'm Chief Inspector Flecker and this is Sergeant Browning.'

'Ah yes, quite.' Holmes-Waterford shook him by the hand. 'And now, what can I do for you?'

'It's the same old story, I'm afraid,' said Flecker. 'Questions and yet more questions.' To Browning's horror he tugged a whole handful of crumpled envelopes from his pocket and began to look through them in a leisurely manner. 'Firstly, I believe you talked with Mr. Broughton at the Chadwicks' party at the time when he was standing alone by the door, "glaring across the room" as one witness put it, at Mr. Vickers. Did you learn anything of his state of mind at that moment?'

The Colonel looked down and watched his foot play with the fringed edge of the hearthrug. 'Frankly, Chief Inspector, you put me in a very awkward position,' he said. 'You see, Mark Broughton is one of my oldest

113

friends. We were at school together and so forth.'

'Yes, I understand, of course,' said Flecker. 'But you have to remember that this is a murder inquiry and that the sort of attitude some of us may take when a friend's in trouble over his car—or even income tax returns hardly meets the situation. After all, sir, two of your own friends have been killed.'

'Yes, of course you are right; I appreciate all that. But it doesn't make my position any easier,' answered Holmes-Waterford.

'I imagine,' said Flecker, 'that Mr. Broughton was in a bad temper on Friday evening.'

'Well, yes.' Holmes-Waterford's voice was grave. 'I'm very much afraid you're right.'

'Did you discuss Mr. Vickers' behaviour?'

'Yes.'

'Was Mr. Broughton annoyed with his presence at the party?'

'Yes.'

'Did he say so?'

'Yes.'

Flecker grinned. 'Can you remember the actual words he used? If so, please repeat them. If not, I'd like the substance of the conversation.'

Once again the Colonel became intensely preoccupied with the fringe of the hearthrug. Flecker waited patiently. 'To the best of my remembrance,' said Duggie Holmes-Waterford at last, 'Mr. Broughton said he would like to wring Vickers' bloody neck—But,' he added hastily, 'knowing him as I do, I recognized it as a figure of speech.

I knew he was simply letting off steam.'

'Did he say anything else? About the hunt for instance?'

'Oh, something rather childish about telling Vickers to take his infernal money to the Shires.'

'That, of course, is the point,' said Flecker. 'There are plenty of packs of hounds which would have been delighted to have Mr. Vickers, and this "hunt quarrel", as my colleagues christened it, was really a storm in a teacup.'

'Exactly,' said Duggie Holmes-Waterford heartily. 'You've put it in a nutshell. There was nothing there for two sane, grown-up men to quarrel over and for Vickers, whose time must have been very largely taken up with training for the Olympics, it was absurd. But I don't think it was the hunt itself he was so taken with. I think it was its proximity to a certain lady.'

'You mean Miss Chadwick?'

Duggie Holmes-Waterford laughed uneasily. 'There's no hiding anything from you, Chief Inspector.'

'Have you any idea how deeply they were attached?' asked Flecker.

'No idea at all. All I know, was that the gentleman was very obviously smitten and that the lady appeared to enjoy his company.'

'And I imagine that Mr. Broughton bitterly resented this?'

'Do I *have* to answer that?' asked Duggie Holmes-Waterford.

'No, sir,' said Flecker, sorting through his envelopes. 'Did you know Mrs. Broughton well?'

'Yes, very well indeed. In fact I think I might describe myself as one of her old flames. We've all three been good friends for many years. When they married I was Mr. Broughton's best man.'

'Do you know why Mrs. Broughton started drinking?'

Holmes-Waterford's eyes returned to the hearthrug. 'Does anyone ever know why these things happen? One can't pinpoint a single incident and say this, or that, made anyone drink. No, it's a snowball of incidents growing larger and larger as the years roll by, and then one day— well, I suppose it just becomes too big to be borne, so you drink to forget it or at least to deaden the pain.'

'Yes, but what sort of incidents?' asked Flecker.

'Well, Mr. Broughton's a very good fellow, but he's exceptionally keen on those hounds. And it's all very well, you know, but women like a little attention even if they are wives. Then he never gave her a child. Well, I know that a lot of women don't want them nowadays; they've too many other interests. But Mrs. Broughton wasn't like that. She wasn't interested in world affairs, or politics or committees for this and that.'

There was a silence, then Flecker put his envelopes in his pocket. 'There are still a lot of questions I'd like to ask you, sir,' he said. 'But I'm afraid I simply must go now as I have an appointment with the Chief Constable. Anyway, thank you very much for your help; I'll come and see you again, if I may.'

'Well, yes, any time, Chief Inspector,' said Duggie Holmes-Waterford, ringing the bell for Gold.

'Oh dear, oh dear,' said Browning, when they were in the car again. 'Those poor kids.'

'What poor kids?' asked Flecker.

'Young Deborah and Jonathan, of course. They're very fond of Mr. B., you can tell it from the way they talk. It's Uncle Mark does this and Uncle Mark says that. Poor little nippers, bad enough having your mum and dad killed by the Mau-Mau without having your uncle hanged for scuppering your aunt.'

'Well, that hasn't happened yet,' Flecker told him. 'You'd better step on it,' he added. 'We're going to be late.' And he pulled out his envelopes and began to rearrange them in a new sequence.

Browning looked disapprovingly at the confusion on Flecker's knees. 'If you must use those old things instead of a notebook I'd better get hold of some rubber bands to keep them tidy.' Flecker, chewing reflectively at the stump of a pencil, said nothing until they reached the police station, when he remarked that he wouldn't be long and bade Browning go and get himself a cup of tea.

Superintendent Fox, who was waiting with the Chief Constable in his office, looked reproachfully at his watch as the Chief Inspector came in. But the gesture was lost on Flecker, who was still deep in thought.

'Well, Chief Inspector, got our man for us?' asked the Chief Constable jovially. 'We're expecting great things of you, you know; we country chaps are all agog to see how you Londoners do it.'

Flecker pushed back his hair. 'I've unearthed a few more facts, sir, mostly irrelevant, and a great deal of extremely relevant gossip. Have you heard from Anstruther?'

'Oh yes, he's been down, removed "certain organs" and taken them back with him—a grisly business,' said the Chief Constable.

'We got his O.K. to send Vickers' body to London,' added Fox. 'The family were being extremely difficult over the delay; I understand the funeral takes place on Friday.'

'And the inquest on Mrs. Broughton is tomorrow morning?' asked Flecker.

'Yes, but it won't be necessary for you to attend unless you want to; we'll send someone along—probably Hollis,' Fox told him.

'Good,' said Flecker. He produced his envelopes, now in some sort of order, and went on. 'One of the most interesting points which has emerged is that Mr. Broughton knew Vickers was to attend the party; he'd been told in case he had any violent objection to meeting him they had both been invited before the question of a joint mastership came up. So far, he and the Chadwicks are the only people who definitely knew Vickers was expected.'

'You've got that in black and white, have you?' asked Fox. Then he turned to the Chief Constable. 'It looks as though Hollis was right.'

'If so, I've got some nice lines in red herrings,' Flecker told them. 'Mr. Denton, the vet, has a first-class motive for the first murder as his wife was seduced—as he puts it—by Vickers last autumn. He would have had opportunity for committing the crime as well as access to and a knowledge of poisons—though nothing in the arsenic line appears to be missing from Marley and Skinner's surgery. The only point in his favour, so far as the first murder is concerned, is that he didn't expect to meet Vickers at the party. For the second murder his motive would have to be a cover-up, but it seems quite feasible that Mrs. Broughton saw something going on. The opportunity for Denton, or for anyone other than Mr. Broughton, to carry out the second murder, seems small. However, Denton was working on Saturday and Sunday; though he says Rollhurst was the nearest he went to Lapworth.'

'Mrs. Broughton was an inside job,' said Fox. 'No doubt about that.'

'Are you getting Broughton to talk?' asked the Chief Constable. 'Hollis couldn't get a reasonable word out of him. Fox here got permission to search, but not much else, did you, Superintendent?'

' "You can turn the whole bloody place upside down, for all I care," was what I got. I took it as permission to conduct a search.' A glint of humour enlivened Fox's stolid face.

'He was quite co-operative this morning,' said Flecker. 'I expect he's calmed down. He seemed to be under the impression that his wife had killed Vickers and then committed suicide.'

'He's taken long enough to that one up,' remarked Fox.

'Where do we go from here?' the Chief Constable asked Flecker.

'Well, sir,' said Flecker. 'I'm going to pay Commander Chadwick a visit and make further investigations into who might possibly have discovered that Vickers was to be at the party. As the Superintendent said, that's rather a damning point. For the future, I'm not too sure. I'd very much like Anstruther's report; it should give me a solid fact or two to work on. The case we're building up at the moment is based on probability; we've very little hard evidence.'

'Well, they died of arsenic poisoning, Broughton's lost a tin of arsenic and he had the opportunity in both cases. Those look like facts to me,' argued Fox.

'They *look* like related facts and I'm hoping that Anstruther's report will tell us whether they are.'

'He won't find that tin of weedkiller for you,' said Fox.

The Chief Constable asked, 'Is there anything we can do for you, Flecker? You don't want any ponds dragged or door to door inquiries made?'

'Not yet,' Flecker answered. 'I may start bothering you for help tomorrow, sir.'

'Right. Well, just let us know when you want us, we're always here,' said the Chief Constable, reverting to his official tone.

Flecker got to his feet. 'Thank you, sir, I will—and you'll let me know the moment Anstruther's report comes through,' he added turning to Fox.

'I will, but I don't think it's going to tell us much we don't know already,' answered the Superintendent. 'Hmm, not getting on very fast,' he went on, as the door closed behind Flecker. 'I'm not sure we wouldn't be better

120

off with Hollis now. It strikes me, sir that there's not such a vast difference between our provincial chaps and the Yard after all.'

'Give him a chance,' said the Chief Constable. 'After all, Fox, he's only been here twenty-four hours.'

Flecker found Browning waiting for him in the entrance hall of the police station, chatting happily to the constable behind the inquiry desk. 'Ready, sir?' he asked.

'Yes, next stop Hazebrook. I hope you're going to see the inside of your dream cottage.'

'I suppose no one thought of offering you a cup of tea?' said Browning as they got in the car.

'No,' answered Flecker, 'but it doesn't matter. I'm quite used to doing without.'

'You do without too many meals,' grumbled Browning. 'And when you do eat, you shovel it down anyhow, thinking of something else.'

Flecker laughed. 'Well, you can't say I look exactly emaciated on it.'

'No, that's true enough, but it's a wonder to me you keep as fit as you do. One of these days you'll find you've got ulcers.'

'Nonsense, the devil looks after his own,' said Flecker, producing his envelopes.

'Oh, I've got a nice rubber band for you.' Browning felt in his pocket. 'Here you are, I begged it off the station sergeant.'

'Thanks,' said Flecker, putting it round his wrist.

CHAPTER THIRTEEN

AT A QUARTER TO FOUR on Wednesday afternoon Mark telephoned Elizabeth Chadwick and asked if he might bring the children over to tea.

'Today? Yes, of course, Mark. We'd love to have you; but I don't promise there'll be much to eat.'

'We're all off our feed,' Mark answered, 'so that won't matter. Provided the car starts, we'll be with you in a quarter of an hour. Are you sure that's all right?'

'Positive,' said Elizabeth and turned, as she put back the receiver, to call for Hilary. Together they dashed to the kitchen to see what they could find to eat.

'Buttered toast,' suggested Hilary. 'There isn't time to boil eggs for sandwiches.'

'Here's a whole packet of chocolate biscuits,' said Elizabeth. 'We're not going to do too badly. So like Mark to ring up at the last minute.'

The Broughtons arrived as the kettle boiled.

'The car started then,' said Elizabeth as she opened the front door.

'Yes,' Mark answered. 'I hadn't used it since Friday, so I had me doubts. Still, we could have come in the flesh van.'

Deborah said, 'Ugh!' but not in her usual spirited tones and Elizabeth, looking from her to Jon, thought, Oh dear, Mark hasn't managed to keep this away from you, you're both frightened out of your wits. 'Come in,' she said aloud. 'Isn't it freezingly cold? We decided to have tea in the drawing-room, even though there's so many of us; the dining-room's icy.'

Hilary came in with the teapot in one hand and the buttered toast in the other, 'Hullo, all,' she said and noticed in a brief glance that Mark was wearing a black tie and looked pale and drawn.

'Charlie thought he might be late, so we're not going to wait for him,' said Elizabeth. 'Do sit down, Mark, and stop behaving like a visitor.'

'Sorry.' Mark sat down hastily. 'I'm having doubts as to whether I'm *persona grata* or not.'

'Don't be silly.' Elizabeth's voice was sharp. 'Have some buttered toast and, if you can't think of anything sensible to say, keep quiet.'

Mark grinned. 'May I take those few kind words as a vote of confidence?'

'You may,' Elizabeth told him. And Hilary said, 'I'll second it.' Deborah was looking from one to the other in an attempt to fathom the conversation, but Jon, aware of the more reassuring atmosphere, had already begun to eat.

'Has the Scotland Yard detective been to see you yet?' Elizabeth asked Mark.

'Yes, we met this morning.'

'How did you get on with him?' asked Elizabeth.

'Well,' Mark answered slowly, 'much to his surprise, I didn't throw him out. I don't think I even swore at him. He seemed quite grateful; I think he must have had alarming reports of my behaviour from the local man.'

'Hollis,' said Elizabeth. 'He's a frightful brute; he annoyed me and I'm not easily annoyed.'

'Hollis couldn't bear us,' said Hilary. 'We drove him

mad with our feminine chatter. At least Chief Inspector Flecker *likes* us to talk.'

'Nan approves of him,' announced Jon through a mouthful of buttered toast. 'She says he's a nice young man. She told him all about Mrs. Tucker and the soup. The Sergeant's horsey; he spent the whole morning in the yard and he didn't seem to be doing much detecting. He finished up in the saddle room reading the pony club book; he said that he couldn't make "head nor tail" of dressage. But he was quite good on the points of the horse, wasn't he, Deb?'

'Yes. And he didn't seem to like being a detective much; he said he'd rather hunt foxes than murderers.'

'I haven't met the Sergeant yet,' said Elizabeth. 'But, like Nan, I thought the Chief Inspector a nice young man. He seemed very earnest; I don't think he'll clap us into jail for nothing, like that nasty Hollis was dying to do.'

Mark cleared his throat. 'This new chap specializes in cosy chats; they always go down well with the ladies.'

'What I want to know,' said Jon, 'is what's going to happen if our two private policemen are still following you about when we start hunting again. Do you think they'll follow hounds in the patrol car?'

Mark grinned. 'I'll offer to mount them,' he said. 'I'll give one of them Killarney and with any luck he'll be put down on the way to the first draw.'

'We could meet at Farley crossroads, bang in the middle of the vale,' said Jon. 'And if you gave the other one Magic he'd be bound to fall in the brook even if he survived the other fences.'

'And we could give Killarney twenty pounds of oats for several days beforehand,' suggested Deb. 'Just to make sure.'

'And I'll ride Silhouette, just to make sure they can't stay with me across the vale,' added Mark.

'Are you being shadowed then?' Elizabeth tried to sound as flippant as her guests.

'Not exactly shadowed,' said Jon. 'They don't try to conceal their presence or wear disguises or anything; they just sit outside the house quite openly.'

'Waste of the ratepayer's money,' said Mark, avoiding Elizabeth's eye.

'Nan likes it,' Deb told them. 'She says that at least no one can murder us.'

'There's something in that,' agreed Mark.

There was a knock on the front door as he spoke and Elizabeth noticed that both the children jumped at the sound. Hilary got up.

'It's not Charlie, he just walks in the back way; besides I haven't heard the car,' said Elizabeth.

There were voices in the hall and then Hilary reappeared.

'Scotland Yard again,' she said. 'They want to see Papa. They say they don't mind waiting.'

'Oh, curse them. Well, they'd better wait in the dining-room, hadn't they, Mark?' asked Elizabeth.

'I don't mind,' answered Mark. 'I ain't afeared. If they're going to wait for Charlie you'd better give them some tea.'

'Oh, bring them in here then, Hilary. They'll freeze in the dining-room and perhaps they'll tell us if there's any news.'

Mark got up as the two detectives came in.

'Good evening,' they said together, blinking a little after the dark outside. 'We didn't mean to interrupt a tea-party,' Flecker added apologetically. 'Wouldn't you rather we went away and came back later? We could easily, we're only staying at Lollington.'

'Not at that dam' awful pub?' asked Mark.

'The Dog and Duck, yes,' said Flecker.

'There's only one good thing about that place,' Mark told him, 'and that's the yard. It's big enough for hounds *and* horses, which is more than you can say of most of the places where we meet. The brewery want to pull the old pub down and build something in stockbrokers' Tudor, but the county council won't have it. Colonel Holmes-Waterford's on something called the planning committee and he told me. Have you been in that appalling saloon bar? They've made an abortive attempt to modernize it with brownish tiles.'

'We usually eat in the saloon bar,' said Flecker ruefully. 'God!'

'Hilary's making some fresh tea,' said Elizabeth.

'Shall I fetch some more cups and plates?' offered Deborah.

'Yes please, Debby, unless Hilary's already got them,' answered Elizabeth.

Mark, standing on the bricks in front of the fireplace, leaning with one arm on the chimneypiece, said, 'I've got a bone to pick with you, Chief Inspector.'

'Oh?' Flecker looked at him inquiringly. 'What about?'

'You never told Nan I didn't want any lunch; it caused a major incident. Everyone thought that I was dead. We had tears.'

'Oh dear, I am sorry,' said Flecker. 'I forgot all about it. My memory's appalling.'

'I'm terribly absent-minded too,' said Elizabeth. 'And Mark, you're not all that reliable yourself.'

'There is also a long yellow garment in my office,' Mark went on, ignoring Elizabeth. 'I'm not much of a detective, but I strongly suspect that it's the Chief Inspector's muffler.'

'Oh, and we've got the Chief Inspector's gloves,' said Hilary, coming in with the teapot. 'He left them here last night.'

Browning looked reproachfully at Flecker. 'I'll have the gloves please, miss,' he said to Hilary. 'Otherwise they'll be left here again.'

' "Who is on my side? Who?" ' asked Flecker sadly.

'You ought to have been brought up by Nan,' Jon told him. ' "A place for everything and everything in its place," ' he added in falsetto accents. 'She gets *livid* with us if we leave our clothes about.'

'My mother always said that too,' Flecker answered. 'And she used to say, "Where you put it, there it'll be", as well. *And* she got livid, but none of it had the desired effect.'

'His mother wanted him to be a parson,' said Browning, who always regarded Flecker's near miss at the church with great pride.

'And why weren't you a parson?' asked Elizabeth,

looking at Flecker and passing cups of tea to all the wrong people.

Flecker pushed hopelessly at his hair. 'Because I fell in love during my first term at Oxford,' he answered. 'And being young and foolish and possessed of high principles, I insisted on marrying the girl. Then I couldn't wait five years for an income so I abandoned theology and joined the police.'

'You hadn't much of a vocation, then?' said Elizabeth.

'No, none at all. My mother didn't believe in them. She was a remarkable woman in many ways—a north-country miner's daughter. She decided that my eldest brother, Henry, should read law and he did, very much against his will; but he's done frightfully well. John wanted to teach, but he was intimidated into being a doctor and now he's a very successful heart specialist. I'm the black sheep.'

'Was the rash marriage a success?' asked Elizabeth.

'Mummy, really!' said Hilary. And Mark said, 'Elizabeth, you're the limit. Stop prying into the Chief Inspector's private affairs. Don't tell her anything,' he advised Flecker. 'She's Auntie Maudie, or someone, to one of those appalling magazines for women. She'll dissect your marriage on her problem page.'

'Well, it wasn't really a problem,' said Flecker. 'Marrying an undergraduate was a step up. Being married to a constable on the beat wasn't, and I didn't make a very good husband.'

'And police hours are enough to break up any home,' grumbled Browning.

'What a shame,' said Elizabeth to Flecker.

128

Hilary got up. 'I must go and feed the horses,' she announced.

'We'll help you,' said Deb, looking at Jon.

'Will we?' Jon shuddered. 'It's jolly cold out there.'

'Yes,' Deb spoke emphatically. 'Come on.' And Jon went without more ado. Flecker, watching Mark, saw that he was following Hilary with his eyes as she left the room. His face was still expressionless. He could be concealing a multitude of sins, thought Flecker, or there might be no more than showed in the heavy-eyed pallor—just grief and strain. As the door closed Mark caught his eye and returned his speculative gaze unflinchingly. Elizabeth, becoming aware of the atmosphere, said, 'For goodness' sake sit down, Mark, you're both acting as a firescreen and looking forbidding.'

'Sorry,' Mark answered and sat obediently.

'More tea, anyone?' Elizabeth asked into the silence which followed. 'More cake, chocolate biscuits?' The three men shook their heads. Elizabeth turned towards Flecker. 'How's the case going, Chief Inspector?' she said easily. 'Any new developments?'

'Nothing very startling. Our pathologist hasn't bestirred himself yet. The mills of justice grind slowly—'

Silence fell again, but this time it was broken by Browning. 'Did Mr. Broughton say that you wrote for one of the women's magazines, madam?' he asked Elizabeth. 'Mrs. Browning's a great reader; she has her book regularly every week. She'd be very amused to hear that I've met one of the writers.'

'I write for rather a dull one, *Women of the World.*

129

You can have a copy for Mrs. Browning if you like.' She crossed the room to fetch one. 'I write under my maiden name,' she went on, 'but you'll know my piece because there's a frightful photograph of me trying to look gracious and not succeeding.'

Browning was thanking Elizabeth when Hilary's head appeared round the door. 'Could we have the Chief Inspector in the kitchen for a minute or two?' she asked. They all looked round at her in surprise.

'Yes, of course,' said Flecker, getting to his feet.

'What's going on now?' asked Mark.

'Nothing much,' Hilary told him. 'It's all under control.'

'Do you want me?' asked Elizabeth.

'No, only the Chief Inspector.'

Flecker went out and Mark and Elizabeth looked at each other in baffled silence.

'Do you think there's been another murder?' asked Elizabeth.

'I shouldn't worry, madam. Probably the children have thought of something,' said Browning soothingly. And then they sat in silence, Browning turning the pages of Elizabeth's magazine, Mark, nodding in his chair, practically asleep and Elizabeth worrying over her husband's late return and wondering where all this misery and violence would end.

CHAPTER FOURTEEN

MARK WAKENED ABRUPTLY when Flecker came back into the drawing-room. 'Hell!' he said, rubbing his eyes. 'Elizabeth, why didn't you kick me on the shins or throw something at me?'

'I thought a sleep would do you good,' she answered. 'And this is hardly a time to bother about party manners. Well, Chief Inspector?'

Flecker crossed the room and looked down at Mark, 'We seem to have found your arsenic, Mr. Broughton,' he said.

'Oh; where?'

'I understand that it is at present concealed in the sleeping compartment of a hutch, occupied by a ferret, name of Rasputin,' said Flecker with an unnaturally straight face.

'*What?*' demanded Mark loudly as he sprang to his feet. 'Do you mean to tell me that Deb and Jon have had that blasted stuff the whole time?'

'I understand they took it from the shelf in the garden shed on Saturday after hunting and handed it over to Rasputin for safe keeping,' said Flecker quietly.

'And I've been cudgelling my miserable brain till I've nearly gone mad,' roared Mark. 'God! They're going to get the rough side of my tongue.'

He started for the door, but Flecker reached it first and barred the way.

'Now then, sir,' he said. 'They're pretty scared and worried by what they've done as it is. Anyway, they only did it on the spur of the moment and they've been trying to find someone to consult ever since. They even lay in wait for Hollis, but apparently he passed by on the other side. Go and sit down, sir, please.'

Mark scowled at him. 'Your mother was wrong,' he said. 'You should have been the headmaster of a prep. school—little boys, eight to twelve, are just about your line.' But he turned obediently and went back to his chair.

Flecker turned to Browning. 'Will you take the children over to Lapworth in the car,' he said. 'They'll show you the hutch and control the ferret. Treat the tin gently, I'd like whatever prints there are. Oh, and if Miss Chadwick's willing, I should take her along too.'

'Right, sir,' said Browning briskly.

'Drive carefully,' Elizabeth called after him.

'If anyone's to blame for this it's Captain Bewley,' said Flecker as he sat down. 'Do you remember Jon giving you a message from Bewley on Saturday evening? He says that you were feeding hounds at the time.'

'Yes,' answered Mark, casting his mind back. 'I remember that he and Deb both looked very worried. He said that Vickers had been murdered and that Bob had had a detective round who knew all about what is now called the "hunt quarrel", but nothing about arsenic.'

'No, they didn't mention the arsenic to you. Apparently Bewley said, "If he's got any arsenic about tell him to get rid of it pronto", so they decided to do that for you.'

'I'll wring Bob's neck next time I see him,' said Mark ferociously.

'You needn't bother. I'll speak to him about it

tomorrow.'

'A lot of good that'll do,' said Mark. 'Bob hasn't a better nature to appeal to.' Then he asked, 'Well, do I stop being suspect number one?'

'Well,' answered Flecker, to be frank, I'm afraid not.'

'But there were other people with grievances against Vickers,' protested Mark. 'Now that you've found my arsenic why shouldn't I move down one for a change?'

Flecker looked at Elizabeth. 'Is this all right, Mrs. Chadwick?' he asked. 'I didn't mean to turn your house into a temporary police station.'

'Quite all right,' answered Elizabeth. 'After all, the murderer used my house and I should like to have the ghosts laid.'

'Well in that case I'll just get my notes; I left them in my overcoat pocket,' said Flecker. 'Oh, no I didn't,' he added as he reached the door. 'Here they are.' And he produced them, now in a tidy bundle, from his hip pocket. 'I'm going to be honest with you, Mr. Broughton,' he said, as he came back to the fire. 'And it's sometimes difficult to be honest and tactful at the same time.'

'Fire ahead,' said Mark, with a grin at Elizabeth. 'I'll take my pill without any jam.'

'Do be serious, Mark,' Elizabeth told him. 'Mr. Flecker's doing his best for us, and it's a serious matter.'

'Don't worry, I'm serious enough,' Mark answered grimly. It's *my* wife who is dead and *my* neck that's in danger. But finding that tin of weedkiller has cleared the air a bit; at least I don't suspect myself now.'

Finding that weedkiller doesn't make so *very* much

difference,' said Flecker, 'except of course that it saves me the trouble of looking for it. You see from my point of view much the same possibilities have to be taken into account. You could easily have helped yourself to a spoonful or two at any time and then just waited your opportunity—'

'My opportunity,' interrupted Mark in exasperated tones. 'My opportunity to rush off to a party with my pockets full of arsenic and poison Vickers because he'd suggested he'd like to be joint master of the hounds. Oh for heaven's sake, man, don't start that again—it's such *nonsense*.'

Flecker said, 'In the police we are taught to search for the concrete rather than the abstract; the method, rather than the motive. But in this case so many of the suspects have had equal opportunity and would all have used more or less the same method, consequently I am driven back to motives. The joint mastership question could have been a contributory factor, especially if you were a fanatic over your hounds—which I don't think you are. But I've afraid I've heard of a much more convincing motive for you than that.' He could see both Mark and Elizabeth from where he sat and watched their faces as he went on: 'The suggestion is that you have been fond of Miss Chadwick for several years and when you saw Vickers was making headway with her you killed him, and then Mrs. Broughton, because they stood between you and Miss Chadwick.'

Mark's face only hardened, but Elizabeth's wore a look of horror. 'Oh, *no*,' she protested.

134

'I've got some nice friends if they all rush off to the police suggesting that sort of thing,' said Mark bitterly. 'What do you want me to do?' he asked Flecker. 'Deny that I'm fond of Hilary? Of course I can't. I can't truthfully say that there haven't been occasions when I wished I were free. Of course I hated Vickers' guts, but that doesn't make me a murderer.'

'No, I know it doesn't,' answered Flecker. 'I realize your predicament, but I've got to suspect everyone until I find the murderer. Do you want me to go on being honest, or would you prefer some tact?'

'Go on, let's have it and get it over,' said Mark wearily.

'Well, you knew that Vickers was to be here on Friday evening. Do you remember Commander Chadwick telling you?'

'Yes, he asked if I *minded*, I don't know what the hell he expected me to say to that.'

'That knowledge meant that you could have come prepared. Then you stayed as far away from Vickers as possible, which would be the obvious thing for the murderer to do, until you said you must go and find your wife; that is the time when you could have committed the murder. You must have had to be very quick; but then whoever did it must have been quick, and prepared to run an enormous risk.'

'But Chief Inspector,' said Elizabeth, 'if Mark was committing murder in order to marry Hilary surely he wouldn't have done it in his future mother-in-law's drawing-room?'

'Was he expecting to meet Vickers anywhere else? Or

135

would it have been his only opportunity to poison him at a party? In some ways it was a good idea to do it at a party; it has made things very difficult to prove. And then murderers never expect to be found out—at least those who premeditate don't.'

Neither Elizabeth or Mark had anything to say, so Flecker shuffled his notes and went on. 'Now we come to the second murder. Well, there are undoubtedly other suspects here, for anyone who took the opportunity to kill Vickers at the party may have wished to silence Mrs. Broughton. If you didn't poison your wife, you must see that we've got to discover how she came to have that bottle of gin. You say you had no visitors on Saturday or Sunday, yet somehow that bottle got in. Anyway, you were out hunting on Saturday—how do you know no one called?'

'I asked Nan,' Mark answered. 'She said she hadn't seen a soul all day.'

'Except for the baker's roundsman, the postman and probably the butcher's boy,' said Flecker sceptically.

'Still, they wouldn't have poisoned Clara.'

'No, but they might have left a parcel.'

'Then Nan would have known about it.'

'Not if they met Mrs. Broughton in the garden.'

'They all knew about my wife's drinking,' said Mark, avoiding Flecker's eye. 'It was common knowledge; everything was always done through Nan. Besides she was— well, what Nan called "poorly" on Saturday, she didn't go out.'

'What about Sunday then?' asked Flecker.

'No one delivers anything on Sundays.'

'Newspapers?' suggested Flecker.

'Yes, they're brought by a boy of about thirteen, who invariably leaves the *News of the World* instead of the *Sunday Times.*'

'He could still have left a parcel,' insisted Flecker.

'Not without Nan seeing it,' said Mark obstinately.

'And you're certain that none of the people who were here on Friday evening came near you?'

'They certainly didn't come near me personally, and Nan is sure that my wife saw no one.'

'You didn't have Mr. Denton to look at a horse or a hound? Mrs. Denton didn't drop in with some animal medicine or to collect anything that her husband had left behind?'

'No. Well, not to my knowledge anyway,' answered Mark.

'You can see why you're still my chief suspect,' said Flecker.

Mark got up and leaned against the chimneypiece. 'It really is the most bloody situation,' he said.

'I call that an understatement,' said Elizabeth miserably.

Mark looked down at her. 'Don't worry about Hilary. I'm not going to involve her in any way. I've never said a word to her, Elizabeth. Well, there was nothing much to say, was there? If she'd been someone else's daughter I might have set up a separate establishment, but as it was I couldn't do a bloody thing.'

'I'm not blaming you,' Elizabeth told Mark. 'I'm protesting at the bludgeoning of chance. What are you going to do, Chief Inspector, if you don't find *any* definite proof?'

'Oh, we'll solve it eventually,' answered Flecker. 'The statistics are with us. I always go through a banging my head against a brick wall stage, unless a crime is perfectly obvious.'

'I know Mark could never have done this sort of a murder, with poison,' said Elizabeth. 'You'll have to try some illogical method, Chief Inspector; a shot at random, an intuitive leap in the dark.'

'I put my trust in inconsequent groping,' Flecker answered. 'Don't worry yourself over it, Mrs. Chadwick, that's what the ratepayers keep me for. That sounds like a car.'

'Yes,' agreed Elizabeth. 'I wonder if it's the children coming back?'

They listened and in a few moments knew by the sound of voices that it was the children. Browning came in first. 'We got it all right, sir,' he said. 'No casualties either. Old Rasputin'll sleep a bit more comfortably tonight; he'll have room to stretch out.'

Deb and Jon came in and stood looking rather apprehensively at Mark. He managed to produce a smile for them.

'It's all right,' he said. The Chief Inspector tells me you're nothing but a couple of crazy mixed-up kids— Ought to go home,' he added looking at his watch. 'We came to tea, not for the night.'

'Oh we can't go *yet*,' protested Deb. 'We've only just got back. Besides we must help Hilary wash up.' And with a virtuous air she began to collect crockery.

'All right,' said Mark. 'Five minutes.'

The washing up was barely under way when Commander Chadwick came in by the back door.

'Hullo ,' he said. 'We seem to have a large staff.'

'We've had Scotland Yard to tea,' Hilary told him, 'as well as Mark and these two. Scotland Yard are waiting to see you. Would you like a cuppa before you become involved?'

'No thanks, I had one in Melborough. Where's your mother?'

'In the drawing-room, talking to the coppers.'

Charlie met Mark at the drawing-room door. Mark said, 'Good evening, Charlie. I came to tea, but I'm just going; if I can persuade my family to leave your kitchen.'

Charlie answered, 'Oh, hullo, Mark,' and then stood in silence, unable to think of anything appropriate to add.

Elizabeth took charge. 'Go and talk to Chief Inspector Flecker,' she said to her husband. 'He's been waiting hours. I'll see Mark out.'

'I'm sorry you've waited "hours",' said Chadwick, looking at Flecker. 'But it's quite easy to telephone first and make an appointment.'

'Yes, of course,' answered Flecker, noticing that the Commander was the same height as himself though of a much lighter build. He could see little resemblance to Hilary in the severe blue eyes and straight, uncompromising mouth. 'Still, we haven't been wasting our time; both Mrs. Chadwick and Mr. Broughton have helped us a lot. Now I'm sorry to bother you, sir,' he went on producing his envelopes. 'But there are just one or two questions about the party.'

'You needn't apologize,' Chadwick told him. 'It's your job to ask questions and my duty to answer them.'

'True,' said Flecker. 'Well, first of all, did you tell any one, besides Mr. Broughton, that Mr. Vickers was coming to your party?'

'*I* didn't tell anyone else,' answered Charlie slowly, 'but of course Mark may have done so, or Guy Vickers for that matter. It's also possible that we were overheard, but I don't think so, I told Mr. Broughton at the meet on the previous Tuesday that Guy was coming.'

'But as far as you were concerned only four people—your wife, your daughter, yourself and Mr. Broughton—knew that Vickers was coming?'

'Yes.'

'Good. Now at the party, you had no drinks poured out waiting, I understand; you poured out for each guest as he arrived?'

'Yes, when I knew what he wanted to drink.'

'And then you filled up their glasses in the hand, as it were?'

'Yes.'

Flecker glanced at his notes. 'Did anyone mislay a glass during the evening?'

'Not that I know of; no one asked me for a new one.'

'Did anyone seem vague about their ownership? You know the sort of thing that goes on: "Is this mine?"—"Oh, I think so; that one up there's Bob's and I think this must be mine—yours had more in it".'

'No, I didn't hear anything of that sort,' Chadwick answered.

'According to the notes I inherited,' Flecker went on, 'practically everyone drank your cocktail. The exceptions were Mr. Broughton, whisky and Mrs. Chadwick and Miss Brockenhurst, sherry.'

'That's right.'

'Now, can you give me any idea at all on how much they drank? I know it's asking the impossible, but anything you can remember may help me.'

'Well, Bewley put away the most,' said Charlie. 'Every time I looked round his glass was empty. I imagine that five or six cocktails would be a conservative estimate. Mark only had two whiskies, but they were large ones and he didn't stay long. Mrs. Broughton had two cocktails and then I didn't offer her another because she was already rather obviously tight. Denton had three, possibly four, cocktails. Miss Brockenhurst had about three sherries; I was working hard on her because she's inclined to be heavy-going conversationally, but from what my wife said to me afterwards I gather I didn't succeed. Vickers had three cocktails, I think, and so did Colonel Holmes-Waterford. Rather moderate going for both of them, but of course the Colonel didn't stay very long. That leaves my family. My wife had two sherries during the party, but she'd had a glass beforehand. My daughter drank about two and a half cocktails; she was so busy talking I don't think she had much time to drink. I acted as taster, trying each new brew as I mixed it; so I kept my glass in the kitchen, which left me with both hands free while I was

141

pouring out.'

'One thing emerges,' said Flecker, looking at the notes he had made as the Commander talked. 'Everyone had two drinks or more. You're quite certain of that? Because my experience of parties tells me that while everyone hangs on to his first drink, as the drowning man to the proverbial straw, he often leaves his second drink about and sometimes loses his third.'

'I'm quite certain,' Chadwick answered. 'You see, I rather fancy myself as a bartender, so if anyone had refused a second glass I'd have wanted to know the reason why.'

'Well, I won't keep you any longer, sir.' Flecker stuffed his notes into his pocket. 'Thank you very much for all your help . . . Home, James,' he said, as he and Browning went out to the car.

'Finishing early tonight, aren't we?' asked Browning.

'A policeman's work is never done,' said Flecker. 'I've got to meditate on the vagaries of man and you've got to pack. You know how long that takes you.'

'Pack?' asked Browning.

'Yes, we've got to cast our nets a little wider. I want you to pay the Vickers family a visit. Paul, the brother, should be home by now since the funeral's on Friday, and he may be more helpful than his parents. I want you to see if you can establish any more connections between Guy Vickers and our list of possibles. Rout out what you can about Antonia, and learn something of his army life, where he was stationed and so on; Broughton, Bewley and Holmes-Waterford were all soldiers.'

CHAPTER FIFTEEN

IT WAS JUST AFTER MIDNIGHT when Flecker, who was in bed but not really asleep, was startled back to full consciousness by a frantic knocking on his door. 'Come in,' he called, sitting up and switching on the light. Mrs. Gordon's head appeared, curlers glinting metallically among the hennaed hair. 'You're wanted on the phone,' she said breathlessly. 'It's the police and they say it's urgent.'

Flecker got up without a word and began to dress, pulling his clothes on over his pyjamas. Like many dreamers he was cool in an emergency, his habitual calmness remaining undisturbed when his mind was jolted into concentration. He laced his shoes and found his overcoat, torch and gloves before he ran downstairs, followed by the still panting Mrs. Gordon.

'Flecker here,' he said, picking up the telephone.

'Jarvis of the county police, sir. I'm on duty at the kennels at Lapworth. The summerhouse in the garden has just gone up in flames. I thought I'd better let you know.'

'Yes, I'll come over right away.' Flecker put down the receiver and turned to Mrs. Gordon. 'If I'm not back by breakfast time, would you tell Sergeant Browning to carry on as arranged, please?'

'Yes, I'll be sure and tell him that. Don't you worry, I won't forget. Whatever 's made them call you out of bed like this in the middle of the night?' she added as she unlocked the front door. 'Not another murder, I hope?'

but her voice, avid for sensation, belied her words.

'Nothing serious,' Flecker answered, hurrying out.

The night was bitterly cold, but the sky was clear. Flecker, driving to Lapworth as fast as the tortuous roads would allow, blessed the brilliant moon. He could see no sign of fire as he drove down the lane to the kennels, but the moment he left the car he smelt smoke and the warm, friendly odour of burning wood. He hurried round the side of the house and there across the lawn, he could see Mark and Jarvis, wielding pitchfork and axe; dark silhouettes against a background of flames. The summer-house itself was a smouldering ruin and round about it on the grass lay bundles of flaming thatch which the two men had hacked from the roof.

'Good morning, Chief Inspector,' called Mark cheerfully when he caught sight of Flecker. 'You're too late; you've missed all the fun.'

'Good morning, sir.' Jarvis wiped a black and sweaty hand across his black and sweaty face. 'We did what we could, but I'm afraid she's had it.'

'How did it happen?' asked Flecker, looking at Mark.

'Don't ask me,' answered Mark flippantly. 'As a house-holder and ratepayer I shall lay a strong protest against the apparent inability of the police to protect private property.'

'Who gave the alarm?'

'I did,' said Mark. 'I was taking a walk round before I went to bed. I was in the stableyard when I saw a sudden glare in the sky and smelled fire; I shot round here, and then I was going for the hose when I met this chap of

144

yours. Of course Codding has put the hose away for the winter and all the taps are frozen up. We were reduced to buckets and the water butt, otherwise we might have made a better job of putting it out.' He was grinning cheerfully; he had enjoyed the action and felt himself again after days of brooding.

'She didn't half go up with a whoof, sir,' said Jarvis enthusiastically. 'Just as though someone had tipped a can of paraffin over the thatch. And you have a look under that bit of floor, sir; there's a bundle of rags that look as though they never got going. Looks like arson all right.'

Flecker shone his torch under what remained of the floor, but made no comment. 'Did you see anyone about?' he asked Jarvis.

'No, only Mr. Broughton.'

'Had you been round this side of the house at all?'

'Yes, two or three times, sir. But I kept up on the path close to the house; I didn't come down here.'

'There are two battery lamps in the boot of my car,' said Flecker, handing Jarvis his keys.

As the constable hurried away Flecker turned to Mark. 'How long had you been wandering about before you met Jarvis?' he asked.

'About ten minutes I should think. I'd walked round the stables and filled up a couple of empty water buckets before I saw the fire.'

'You hadn't got the dogs with you?'

'No, they'd been barking earlier. I thought it was probably at your man and as I didn't want to wake the place, I left them indoors. They'd all been out once when

145

the children went to bed.'

'Which door did you leave the house by?' asked Flecker.

Mark looked a little shamefaced. 'To tell you the truth,' he said, 'I came out of the office window.'

Flecker looked at him sharply. 'Why?'

'A sudden re-awakening of juvenile irresponsibility,' Mark answered, leaning on his pitchfork and grinning. 'I was tired of finding a policeman on the doorstep every time I went out and, as I didn't know which doorstep he was on, I went out through the window.'

'A pity,' said Flecker.

'Now I'm back in the doghouse, I suppose,' said Mark, looking faintly amused. 'Look here, Chief Inspector, how was I to know someone was going to set fire to my summerhouse? If I had known, my behaviour would have been exemplary and I should have taken care to be having a nice chat with Jarvis when the balloon went up. Besides, why should I burn down my own summerhouse?'

'Why should anyone burn it down?' asked Flecker. He was reproaching himself for not having examined the place before. It was true that he had meant to do so this morning while Mark was at the inquest, but now he had been forestalled. It was also true that it had already been searched by the county police, but their minds had been fixed on arsenic and they might easily have missed some vitally important evidence. What evidence, he asked himself, would need such a wholesale method of destruction? Apart from bodies and bloodstains, the answer seemed to be fingerprints or some small thing that

146

had been dropped and could not be found. But it would have to be very conclusive evidence to be worth the risk of focusing so much attention on the summerhouse. It was possible, of course, that it had been an act of spite unconnected with the murders, or the work of a crank— for Broughton was now getting a good deal of publicity in the daily Press.

'I suppose,' said Flecker, looking up at Mark, 'you *didn't* set fire to it yourself?'

'No, I didn't. And, if I had, I should have let the thing burn down and not helped Jarvis put it out.'

'I don't know about that,' said Flecker. 'Having been caught almost in the act of starting a fire, to pretend you were putting it out would be the most intelligent thing to do.'

'Still, I needn't have been so efficient,' Mark pointed out. 'I could have stood about wringing my hands. I could have wasted a long time waking all the men. I could have telephoned for the fire brigade and, what with a manual exchange and the fire engine having to come from Melborough, the summerhouse would have been ashes before they arrived.'

'You could,' agreed Flecker. 'But on the other hand all those buckets of water will have effectively destroyed any fingerprints.'

'Well, if I can't leave fingerprints in my own summer-house, where can I leave them?' demanded Mark.

'It wasn't your fingerprints I was interested in,' said Flecker as Jarvis came back. 'Now,' he went on, taking one of the lamps, 'if someone wanted to reach the summerhouse without coming down the lane and through the front gate, how would he come?'

'Either through the stableyard,' answered Mark, 'though that means the lane, unless he took a cross-country route from the road—or else from the Langley to Great Lapworth footpath.'

'How do you get here from the footpath?' asked Flecker.

'Down there.' Mark indicated a little path that led away from the lawn through rough grass and shrubs to where a clump of chestnut trees marked the corner of the garden and the beginning of a pasture field.

'We'll have a look down there,' said Flecker. He led the way, shining his lamp on every inch of the ground before him and in the bushes and shrubs on either hand. The ground, frozen hard by the five-day frost, yielded no clue. The shrubs, well cut back, presented no boughs to brush an intruder, no thorns to tear at his clothes. By the chestnut trees a wicket gate led down into the moonlit fields. 'There's the path,' said Mark, pointing across the field. 'There are three stiles between here and the church at Great Lapworth, and at this end there's one out into the Little Lapworth road, about three hundred yards further along than our lane. Then, if you cross the road, you can go on to Langley, but that part of it is a bridle path and there are gates instead of stiles.'

'Neither of you heard a car start either before or after you saw the fire, I suppose?' asked Flecker.

'No,' answered Mark.

'Nor me,' said Jarvis. 'And I think I would have done because sound travels a long way these frosty nights.'

Flecker turned back. 'I'll have a look down there later on,' he said.

They went back to the summerhouse. Several of the bundles of thatch had begun to smoulder again. Mark picked up a bucket and strolled off towards the stables as if to fetch some more water. Flecker turned to Jarvis, who waited expectantly beside him. 'Did you hear Mr. Broughton before you saw him?' he asked.

'Well yes, I think so, sir. I heard what sounded like a bucket kicked over in the stableyard and slipped round there quick; but there was no one about, so I thought it must have been one of the horses. Then I came back round the front and was just going round to the lawn side of the house when I met Mr. Broughton. He said, "The summerhouse is afire; I'm going to fetch the hose", or words to that effect.'

'Did you take a look yourself before you rang me?'

'Oh yes, sir.'

'And the fire was well established?'

'She was burning all right and as I looked she went up with a whoof, just as though someone had tipped a couple of cans of paraffin over the thatch.'

'I suppose,' said Flecker, that you don't remember whether Mr. Broughton smelled of paraffin when you ran into him? He does now, but then so do you. You thought that paraffin had been used to get the fire going—might it have been the smell of it that made the thought of paraffin leap instantly into your mind?'

Jarvis considered Flecker's words for several moments before he answered. 'I wouldn't like to swear to it either way, sir,' he said. 'You see, my young sister's not much of a hand at lighting fires and if mum's back's turned she resorts to the paraffin can; that's how I come to recognize the whoof of it. Singed her eyebrows once, Sis has, but even that hasn't stopped her.'

Mark had returned with the water and was making a determined effort to quench the last vestige of fire. A smell of wet, charred wood pervaded the garden. Without the fire it was very cold and Flecker, salvaging the half-burnt rags from under the summerhouse, was delighted when Mark offered to make tea, remarking maliciously as he did so that he was providing nothing stronger, 'out of deference to police regulations'.

'We'd love some,' Flecker answered, as he put the rags into a paper bag from his pocket. 'Come on, Jarvis.'

As they waited for the kettle to boil Flecker took the opportunity to ask Mark which of the guests at the Chadwicks' party knew of the footpath and of the little gate into his garden.

Mark thought for a moment. 'All the Chadwicks,' he answered. 'Holmes-Waterford, Bewley, but not the Dentons or Miss Brockenhurst so far as I know. We had a lot of parties in the garden at one time but none lately; I think the last was nearly four years ago.'

'However, Mr. Denton comes to the stables quite often, I imagine?' said Flecker.

'Yes, and I sometimes bring him in for a drink. But I can't remember taking him round the garden. Of course, the footpath is plainly marked on the map.'

'Which of the windows look out over the lawn?' asked

Flecker.

'My wife's bedroom and the drawing-room, which we don't use at the moment.'

Flecker began to examine his half-burned rags. They appeared to be the remnants of a sheet and they smelled of paraffin. The least charred part was the hem and he made his way along it, examining it carefully inch by inch, until he came to the corner where a stoutly sewn-on nametape, still intact, bore the word 'Broughton' in blue script. He looked at it for a moment and then sighed as he returned the rags to their paper bag. 'I'll just put this in the car,' he told Mark.

When he came back Deb and Jon had appeared and evidently raided the larder.

'We're having a midnight feast,' Deb told him.

'For which,' said Mark ruefully, 'I shall get a rocket from Nan in the morning.'

'Blame the police,' suggested Flecker, sitting down. 'Our shoulders are very broad. Tell her the Chief Inspector had a lean and hungry look,' he added with a grin at Jarvis, who, now that he had taken off his helmet and washed the grime from his face, was obviously very young and seemed rather ill at ease.

It was a quarter to two when Flecker said that he must go back to work. He rescued Jarvis from Deb, who was giving him long and detailed instructions on what to do if the stables caught fire, and together they walked round the garden and stableyard. It was colder than ever and except for intermittent puffs of wind the only sounds came from the stables, the occasional clink of a bucket or the scrape of hoofs on a loose-box floor as one of the horses got up or lay down.

Having told Jarvis to include the summerhouse in his rounds, Flecker left him to keep his vigil alone and set off across the fields. Out in the open, the moon and frost combined in silvered brilliance, but the hedgerows and trees cast great black shadows over the path to Lapworth, shadows which vibrated eerily as the wind rustled through the frozen twigs. Flecker found himself absurdly tensed; constantly looking round instead of keeping his eyes on the path at his feet.

He examined the three stiles carefully, collecting every bit of wool or cloth which adhered to them, however insignificant looking, and putting it away in an envelope. From Great Lapworth he turned back and, passing below the kennels, continued along the valley to the Little Lapworth road. There he looked for recent signs of a stationary car, tyre marks and patches of oil or water, but found nothing. Feeling warm and energetic he decided to go on to Langley, but he soon regretted his decision for the bridle path, rutted by tractors and poached by many hoofs, was frozen hard and the uneven surface made walking unpleasant. The gates yielded no clues and, when he reached Langley and had to retrace his steps, Flecker felt tired and disheartened. He began to wonder whether he was as good a detective as he was supposed to be and whether Hollis, who sounded like a hustler, wouldn't have completed the case by now. In all his successful cases luck had played a large part; supposing luck deserted him now?

A very alert looking Jarvis spotted him the moment he reached the kennels and came up to report that all was quiet and even Mr. Broughton had gone to bed. They chatted for a time and then Flecker went to work on what was left of the summerhouse. Patiently and methodically he sorted through the charred and sodden mass, laying his finds in rows on the lawn: a charred box containing undamaged croquet balls, two and a half mallets; the metal part of a trowel, sundry remains of deckchairs, all the odds and ends one would expect to find in a summerhouse, plus an empty gin bottle and a quantity of broken glass.

Dawn came, heralded half-heartedly by the depleted cock population of the post-Christmas months, before Flecker had finished. Day followed with the temperature still below freezing and a slight strengthening of the bitter wind. It was just light when finally Flecker straightened up. He was standing by the summerhouse, trying to rub some warmth into his numbed and filthy hands, when something crashed into the bushes below, between him and the chestnuts. He ran down the little path to the gate and cautiously looked out across the field. He did not need the string of boxers and spaniels to tell him that the angular figure, the corduroys and windcheater, the short red hair, belonged to Miss Chiswick-Norton. She was walking very briskly across the field towards the stile which led to the Little Lapworth road and the bridle path to Langley.

Flecker hurried back to the shrubbery. Crawling among the bushes, it took him only a short time to find the missile, a small rusted tin with a tattered label which read: *Atkinson's Weedkiller. Poisonous. Contains Arsenic.* Gathering it up gently in his handkerchief he returned, whistling tunelessly, across the lawn.

CHAPTER SIXTEEN

'SUPPOSE,' said Colonel Holmes-Waterford, as his wife got up from the breakfast table, 'you don't feel like attending the inquest this morning?'

Alicia turned back from the door. Her well-groomed hair, dark and abundant, framed a plump, determined face. Her roundly obstinate chin was tilted for battle. She was a woman who prided herself on her forthrightness.

'Not on your life,' she said. 'I couldn't stand Clara Broughton when she was alive, or Mark, who thinks he's God Almighty because he's master of those tuppenny-ha'penny hounds. And now that they've got themselves into this sordid mess, I'm even less interested. *I'm* certainly not going to gape at Mark because he's a murderer. But don't let me stop you; they're your friends, not mine.'

'The papers have evidently plumped for Mark,' said Duggie Holmes-Waterford pacifically. 'But I don't know that it's a foregone conclusion yet. I see that one of them states that an arrest is imminent, but until that happens I don't think we should cast our votes or weight the scales too heavily against him. The inquest is being held at the police station and I think I shall just look in. After all, having known Mark and Clara so long, I think it's really my duty to go.'

'Duty, my foot! You're just going to gape.'

Duggie stared fixedly at his plate as he struggled to gain

command of his temper. 'I don't think that's quite fair, Alicia,' he said, 'considering all the years I've known Mark.'

' "It's not fair",' Alicia mimicked him. 'If you had any sense you'd drop Mark like a hot brick, not to mention all those boozy Bobs and Steves and your ghastly friends from Sleeches Farm. Daddy's going to think we know some nice people when he reads the Sunday gutter Press,' she added over her shoulder as she marched out of the room.

'But I don't want to go,' said Antonia Brockenhurst for the third time. 'I went to Guy's inquest and that's enough. Anyway, I've got a lot to do.'

'But Annie, you *must*,' Miss Chiswick-Norton protested. 'It's no use running away from these things. We've simply got to face up to it; come along now, be a brave girl.'

'*No*. You can go if you want to. I've got to take Goody Two Shoes out for a couple of hours; I must get her fit if I'm going to race next month. Then there's Grey Malkin's leg to poultice and I've just got to clean out the hens, their house is in a perfectly disgusting state.'

'Poor old Norty'll have to go alone then,' said Miss Chiswick-Norton dolefully. Norty had been her nickname when she served in the A.T.S. and she was as devoted to it as she was to the war years, which had remained her finest hour, despite the passing of more than a decade of peace.

'That's right,' said Antonia, with relief. 'You go and then you can tell me about it afterwards; though I suppose they'll only adjourn it like they did Guy's.'

'You never can tell,' said Miss Chiswick-Norton. 'But don't you worry, dear, Old Norty's not as silly as she lets people think; she works behind the scenes, and, believe you me, everything is going to be all right.'

Antonia Brockenhurst looked at her partner vaguely; then she said, 'Well, I must go and groom Two Shoes. Bring back something for lunch; I'm sick and tired of eggs.'

Stephen Denton knew very well that Sonia had only pretended to be asleep, but he had subscribed to the pretence and got his own breakfast. It was a nice state of affairs he thought, as he ate bacon and eggs without relish. They had done nothing but quarrel since Vickers was poisoned, for, despite her tearful denials, it was obvious that Sonia believed her husband had killed her lover. Every evening since Vickers died, thought Steve, we've rowed. He knew that he was largely to blame; for however good his intentions, he had only to be in the flat half an hour to find himself shouting and storming. Demanding that Sonia should tell him he was a murderer to his face, that she should call the police. He knew he was being unreasonable, but how, he wondered, could one help it? The trouble about marriage was that you learned to know your partner too well; you knew the reservations behind the most emotional protestations of belief, you recognized the judas kiss. The only remedy was to work later and later, to spend a couple of hours in the Coach and Horses, to come home late enough for Sonia to be in bed, to keep up the pretence that she was asleep, and to eat one's dried-up supper in solitude.

Flecker returned to Lollington with just enough time to wash, shave, change his incredibly dirty clothes and eat a hurried breakfast, before taking Browning to catch the London train. Browning was very offended that he had been left out of the adventures of the night and refused to admit Flecker's argument that it was absurd for two people to lose their sleep when one would do. He departed, still disgruntled, and Flecker drove to the police station.

Superintendent Fox seemed friendlier than before. 'Ah, I've got something for you,' he said, producing the report from Anstruther. 'Sodium arsenide, he says.'

Flecker read the report through quickly. 'There's something even more interesting than that,' he said. 'At least, I think so. Can you spare me a couple of men?'

'Two?' Fox looked doubtful. 'We're in the middle of a 'flu epidemic, and we've got to turn the place upside down for this inquest. Wait a minute though, what about Broughton? We don't need to keep a man up there permanently, do we, now that we know it wasn't his weedkiller?'

'I don't know, sir,' answered Flecker thoughtfully. 'Some odd things seem to be going on.'

'I heard you had a spot of bother up there in the night. In fact I telephoned the open Borstal this morning, but they've got their full complement of boys. I'd be inclined to put it down as a coincidence myself. Still, if I send the patrol car round that way and get the local chap to pop up a couple of times a day they ought to be all right. Broughton hasn't showed any signs of running and he's quite capable of dealing with the press himself. What do you want these chaps to do?'

Flecker explained. One was to go round the wine merchants and the off-licence pubs and shops with a list of names and find out which of those mentioned on it dealt where and what they consumed. The other man was to find out where flypapers could be bought. He was to make a note of brands sold and to find out if anyone on the list had been buying them.

'If we could get hold of a few photographs from the local paper or somewhere, it would be a help,' Flecker suggested. 'And the other thing I want,' he went on when Fox had finished making notes, 'is the report of the inquest on a child drowned at Langley three years ago.'

After the inquest on Clara Broughton, a dreary proceeding over which Nan's tears cast an even deeper gloom, Bob Bewley tried to collect the other suspects for a drink in the Coach and Horses. Mark, accompanied by Nan and Codding, had already left; he had dodged the photographers by using a side entrance to the police station and had driven off without a word to any of his friends. Charlie Chadwick's curt, 'Not *now*, Bob,' clearly showed that he thought the suggestion unsuitable, but Bewley, quite unabashed, went on to tackle Duggie Holmes-Waterford.

'Come on, Colonel, you look as though you need one.

It's a medicinal necessity after what we've been through.'

With Alicia's comments still rankling, Duggie refused firmly and looking at Bob, who, in his last good suit was at his most respectable, reflected that the bloodshot eyes and the tinge of purple that discoloured his nose were clear indications of the sort of life the man led. Perhaps Alicia was right; when all this was over he'd drop the local riff-raff and stick to his own sort.

Only Steve Denton consented to drink with Bob and he stipulated that it must be a quick one and only one, out of consideration for his equine and bovine patients.

Bob bought the drinks and led the way to a quiet corner.

'Cheerio,' he said, and then, embarking at once on the topic he wished to discuss—'I don't know how these murders are affecting you, Steve, but I'm being treated in Hazebrook as though I were Crippen himself. The old biddy who comes in once a week to clean up, cowers in corners with chattering teeth and none of my little village girlfriends will even drink with me. I think it's time we put our heads together and sorted it out. The police aren't exactly hurrying themselves and now Clinkerton tells me that Mark's going to let Haines hunt hounds because of the "unfavourable publicity" he's received. That means no hunting worth having, for the poor old chap doesn't go a yard.'

'I'm under a cloud too,' said Steve; 'both with Sonia and with the police. But I don't see what we can do about it. I'm just waiting for them to find the right man. After all, they've got the knowledge, the equipment and any

160

evidence there is.'

'They weren't there when Vickers was murdered,' said Bob. 'If we got everyone together in the Chadwicks' room again, we could sort it out, surely? Vickers couldn't have been poisoned right under our noses without any of us seeing a thing.'

Steve sighed. 'Well, *I'd* be glad enough to have it sorted out.'

'I didn't realize you were having a rough time,' said Bob. 'I thought it was only Mark they were itching to arrest. D'you think he's in the clear?'

'I don't know at all, Bob; but Sonia says the Chief Inspector knows that Mark is interested in Hilary, or Hilary in Mark, whichever way round it is—if it is.'

'That's bad,' said Bob. 'Not that I suppose there's any incriminating evidence to be found, but it's the very fact they're both such souls of honour that makes murder the answer. No one would suspect that old libertine Bob of murdering for love. If he couldn't have one woman he'd have another; married, unmarried, doesn't matter; it's all one to me. But Mark's got very old-fashioned views on holy matrimony. He told me once that illicit amours should be conducted as far away from home as possible; he was very disapproving of what he crudely called my "whoring round the village".'

'Well, you do go a bit far, you know,' Steve said amiably.

Bob laughed. Then, looking more serious, he put his hand on the other's arm. 'Will you get hold of Elizabeth, Steve? Use your well-known charm and persuade her to ask us all there on Saturday evening? She's more likely to do it for you than me. If I suggest it she'll think I've got some shady ulterior motive.'

'I'll do my best to get them together,' said Steve. 'But I'm not sure that I wouldn't rather provide the hospitality myself; the Chadwicks have had enough to put up with. I'll ask Sonia and let you know, Bob.'

'Right you are, but don't take no as answer from any of them. They'll probably jib at first; they seem to have a sneaking feeling that murder isn't the done thing, but really they're all dying for a good gossip. Oh, and I shouldn't ask Mark,' Bob added as Steve got up to go. 'It's a bit too near the funeral.'

Flecker had spent most of the morning in Langley, trying to discover the presents whereabouts of Mrs. Basset, the foster-mother of the drowned child. The village had changed in the last three years. The villagers had left the damp but picturesque cottages overlooking the Meld and migrated to the council-built estate on the hill and, in their wake, the impoverished gentry of the countryside, selling their unheated houses to institutions, had moved in. With one accord they had installed bathrooms and modern kitchens, removed fireplaces of mottled tiles revealing ancient hearths, turned the cabbage patches into lawns and rosegardens. None of them could help Flecker. In the post office he found an old couple who explained that their daughter had gone out for the day and left them in charge. Changing their spectacles they turned the leaves of various rather unbusinesslike-looking exercise books with shaking hands until they came to Mrs. Basset's name and the address to which she had asked that any letters should be forwarded. To Flecker's disappointment it was a London address. Three years was a long time in London, he thought gloomily, and town memories are shorter than country ones. As he thanked the old couple for their help, there was a clattering of hoofs outside the post office and he came out to find Antonia Brockenhurst trying to force a large and excitable-looking horse along the path between his car and the pillarbox, with the evident intention of posting a letter.

'Can I help?' asked Flecker. 'Shall I post it for you?'

'She ought to do it; she's just being perfectly ridiculous,' replied Antonia angrily, and, giving Goody Two Shoes a wallop with her whip, was at once precipitated wildly across the road. 'Stop it, you stupid brute,' she growled as she yanked the mare round.

'Give me the letter, Miss Brockenhurst,' said Flecker in tones of authority, and added, as soon as Antonia had stopped struggling with her horse, 'I've got something you may be able to identify.' He posted the letter and fetched the tin of arsenic from the car. 'Do you recognize this?' he asked, holding it up, and knew at once by her face that she did. Uncertain what to answer she stared woodenly at the tin until Flecker decided to help her out.

'I believe you told the police originally that you had no weedkiller on the farm so far as you knew. This looks ancient enough to have been left behind by a previous tenant,' he suggested.

'Yes, it looks very like the one we found on the window-ledge in the apple shed,' said Antonia guiltily. 'It didn't belong to either of us, though; we'd never set eyes on it before, but it must have been there all along. I suppose it was just that we'd never noticed it . . .'

'Are you and Miss Chiswick-Norton early risers?'

'It depends what you call early,' said Antonia. 'I'm out in the yard about half past seven in the winter. Earlier on hunting days, of course.'

'What about this morning?'

'Oh, my partner was up first this morning. She wanted to go to the inquest so she took the dogs out before breakfast.'

'And what time did you go to bed last night?' asked Flecker.

'Oh, early, about ten o'clock. There hasn't been another murder, has there?'

'No, only a fire this time,' answered Flecker. 'I won't keep you any longer,' he added hastily as Goody Two Shoes began to throw herself about in a series of leaps and bucks.

'Where was the fire?' Antonia shouted above the clatter of hoofs, but Flecker pretended not to hear and waving cheerfully, climbed into his car.

After lunching at the Dog and Duck, Flecker drove to the kennels where the front door was opened to him by Deborah. 'Hullo,' he said cheerfully, you look as though you've been riding.'

'Good afternoon,' Deb answered formally. 'Yes, actually we have. Hilary came out with us and it was absolutely

164

icy.'

'Is your uncle at home?' asked Flecker.

'Yes,' Deb turned and abandoning her poise, bawled at the top of her voice, 'Uncle Mark, the Chief Inspector wants to see you.'

Mark appeared in the passage. 'Really Deb, must you?' he protested. 'No wonder Miss Pinkerton, or whatever the woman's name is, complains.'

Jon's head peered round the sitting-room door. Deborah *must* learn to modulate her voice,' he exclaimed in falsetto accents.

'Come into the office, Chief Inspector,' said Mark, leading the way.

'The family seem to have cheered up,' observed Flecker.

'Yes, they've been out with Hilary; she's very good with them.' Mark sighed.

Flecker said, 'I only want to ask you one question. I heard at this party last Friday you told Mrs. Broughton not to have more than one drink; is that right?'

'Yes.'

'I suppose that you were keeping an eye on her during the party; have you any idea if she did only have one?'

'I didn't keep an eye on her,' answered Mark. 'We'd passed that stage; I used to cross my fingers and hope for the best. I didn't expect my plea for one drink to have any effect, but for some reason she did only have one. She told me so as we left.'

'But mightn't she have just said that to please you?' asked Flecker.

'No, I don't think so. I know that they say that

165

alcoholics are immoral or amoral, whichever it is, but Clara still had certain standards. She'd never lie just to create an effect; she hated vainglorious boasting. Certainly she wouldn't have gone out of her way to tell me that she had had one drink if she'd had two, though she might not have told me the truth if I had asked her how many she'd had. That was why I never did ask her; there was no point.'

'Thank you,' said Flecker. 'Well, that's the lot so far as you're concerned, sir; but d'you think I could see Nan?'

'She's being a bit emotional,' said Mark gloomily. 'And she still suspects me though we've found the arsenic. I don't think she'd have come to Melborough in the car this morning if I hadn't arranged to take Codding as well. But it's up to you, if you like to brave the flood—she's in the kitchen. The more upset she is the harder she works; I'm expecting spring cleaning to start at any minute.'

Flecker found Nan polishing silver.

'That Mrs. Philips is supposed to do it, but you can see it's not 'alf done,' she told him. 'All Mrs. Broughton's lovely things tarnished. Wedding presents and all. And this was Sir Richard's shaving jug. They presented it to him; I forget what it was for now, but he was a very clever man. Oh, a very clever man. I don't know whatever he'd have thought of all this, 'e'd turn in 'is grave if he knew 'alf of what was going on.'

Flecker spoke quickly to avert the threatened tears. 'He'd want us to find out who the murderer was, wouldn't he? I don't want to upset you, but I do need your help; you knew Mrs. Broughton better than anyone.'

'I'll do all I can to 'elp ,' answered Nan.

Flecker pulled out a chair and sat down opposite her at the kitchen table. 'First of all,' he said, producing envelopes and a pencil, 'Mr. Broughton tells me that you are sure no visitors came to the house on Saturday or Sunday. Is that right?'

'That's right. I never saw a soul all day long, except for Mrs. Broughton and Codding. He was in in the morning for 'is elevenses, but he goes off twelve sharp on Saturdays and 'e went over to Kidford on the bus to see 'is sister. Oh, Mrs. Philips came in in the morning and tore around, 'alf doing them bedrooms.'

'No one brought a parcel for Mrs. Broughton?' asked Flecker.

'A parcel? No, that they didn't.'

'You're sure? It's very important.'

'Well, if they 'ad, they'd have given it to me, for she was upstairs poorly all Saturday.'

'Mrs. Philips might have taken it up?' suggested Flecker.

'She never went near Mrs. Broughton. I always did 'er room myself.'

'How did Mrs. Broughton get all that extra gin?' asked Flecker. 'It can't have fallen from the skies. She never went in to Melborough or down to the village pub, did she?'

'No, she never went further than the garden unless 'e took her and that wasn't often.'

'Well, how do you suppose she got hold of all that extra drink?'

'The doctor from the 'ome said she was to have so

much,' Nan explained. ' "You can't cut it of altogether", he says, "but if you don't limit it she'll kill 'erself". Mr. Broughton ordered the right amount each month and then, what he had for 'imself, he kept locked up in the safe in the office. But I used to wonder sometimes 'ow she did get hold of the extra and whether it was 'im. Whether he remembered what the doctor 'ad said, and whether he wanted to be rid of 'er.'

'I see,' said Flecker, gnawing his stump of pencil reflectively. 'Do you remember if Mrs. Broughton went out in the garden on Saturday or Sunday?'

'Not Saturday, she didn't; she was poorly all day. But she went out on Sunday, no coat nor nothing. "You'll catch your death," I told 'er, but she didn't take a bit of notice, not a bit.'

'What time was this?'

'Sunday afternoon. 'E was drinking in the office and the children were out in the stables seeing to them ponies. I was just going to put the kettle on for tea when I noticed she'd gone. I looked out of 'er bedroom window and there she was across the lawn, only half dressed and out in her bedroom slippers, in all that wet grass. By the time I got downstairs she was in the 'all.'

'Was she carrying anything?' asked Flecker.

'Only a little coat. She 'adn't even the sense to put it on.'

'Mr. and Mrs. Broughton never had any children, did they? ' asked Flecker. 'Not even a stillborn one?'

'No, nothing,' Nan answered sadly. 'She wouldn't 'ave one at first. I warned her. "Don't you go interfering with nature", I told her; "no good ever came of it." But she wouldn't listen. She didn't want to settle down straight away; she wanted to have a good time—hunting and going to parties.'

Flecker's last call that afternoon was on Captain Bewley at Hazebrook. He left his car in the road and guided by Bewley's voice swearing viciously at a horse, entered the stableyard. The swearing stopped abruptly when the Captain heard footsteps on the concrete and when his head appeared over the loose-box door he spoke pleasantly and in his usual bantering tones.

'Come to arrest me, Chief Inspector?' he inquired. 'Where's the horsey sergeant?'

'Chasing red herrings,' Flecker answered. 'I won't keep you a moment, sir, but, I've just got a couple of questions. I'd like answered.'

'You're as bad as the Elephant Child,' said Bob. 'But carry on.'

'You gave me a graphic account of how you collected Mrs. Broughton from Mr. Vickers last Friday evening. Now can you remember if she had a glass in her hand?'

'A glass?' said Bob thoughtfully. 'No, I don't think she had. No, wait a minute, it's coming back to me now. She hadn't got a drink at all. I offered to get her one; in fact we had a bit of an argument about it, but she said she'd promised her husband or something. She was a bit inconsequent and I wasn't feeling any too sharp myself. But I am sure about the glass.'

'Good,' said Flecker.

'You don't think she killed Vickers, do you?' asked Bob. 'I suppose that she might have gone a bit shaky up top. She wouldn't have done it in her normal state, she couldn't even bear to see hounds kill.'

'No, I don't think she did it,' answered Flecker. 'I suppose you haven't an alibi from eleven until one last night?'

Bewley laughed. 'Considering that my second wife has recently deserted me, I call that a highly indelicate question. But the answer is no. I was in bed from half-past eleven onwards—alone. What happened last night, anyway?' he asked on second thoughts. 'Not another murder?'

'No, nothing very disastrous,' said Flecker. 'Goodnight,' he called as he made for his car.

From Lollington Flecker telephoned Superintendent Fox. He learned that so far the two men making inquiries for him had found nothing of especial interest. 'This 'flu's holding them up a bit,' Fox told him. 'A lot of the managers are away sick. Still, they hope to be through by the weekend.'

'I shall be going to London tomorrow,' Flecker said. 'I've got hold of an address for Mrs. Basset, but it's three years old. I'll report to the Central Office while I'm there.'

Fox said, 'I don't see what good Mrs. Basset's going to do you when you do find her—still, that's your business. All right, Flecker, I'll hold the fort; let me know when you're back.'

170

CHAPTER SEVENTEEN

CLARA BROUGHTON was buried at Great Lapworth on Friday afternoon. Although the date and time had not been published, they had become known locally and the handful of friends and relations was augmented by a crowd of sensation-seeking visitors from the villages round about.

It was a depressing funeral. Neither Clara's life nor the manner of her going offered any comfort to the mourners, but only Nan's grief was unqualified. The relations could not forget that Clara had been murdered. They looked surreptitiously at Mark—it was usually the husband—and then at his friends.

Mark, though he showed no sign of it, was very conscious of the searching looks and the nudging that accompanied his appearance. His mind was as much on his own predicament as on Clara's tragic end.

Afterwards, Clara's relations refused an invitation to go back to the house, but two or three Broughtons, remembering that blood was thicker than water and that in case the worst came to the worst someone ought to take an interest in the children, decided that it was their duty to accept.

Mark, frigidly aloof, provided whisky and then relapsed into silence. A sniffing Nan produced an enormous meal which no one could eat, while the children, who'd spent the afternoon with Hilary Chadwick, only appeared shortly before their relatives departed.

On Friday evening Steve Denton reached home in time for supper. He found Sonia cooking and, ignoring all that had passed between them, embarked on an outline of Bob Bewley's plan.

'I'm going to do something constructive about these murders,' he told her. 'This misery has gone on long enough. I'm going to ask everyone who was at the party, bar Mark, round for a drink tomorrow evening. I'm sure that between us we ought to be able to help the police, and they don't seem to be getting anywhere by themselves.' He made the idea his own, not because he wanted the credit for it, but because he was certain of Sonia's reflex antagonism if she knew that it had come from Bob.

Sonia said, 'Oh,' and then, after a moment's reflection— 'People in to drinks? The place is in a terrible mess, Steve, and look at my hair. I didn't have it set this week.'

'Nothing like that matters,' said her husband. 'It isn't a party. We shall all be thinking about the murders and not noticing dust, or even your hair, which looks perfectly all right to me.'

'You may be thinking of the murders, but the others won't be; women are such cats.'

After supper Steve telephoned. The Chadwicks, doubtful at first, agreed to come when they heard that it was to be a serious attempt to pool available knowledge and not just a gossipy party. Antonia Brockenhurst had to be persuaded. She said that she was sick and tired of the whole affair and had already told the police everything she could remember about the party. When she finally gave way to Steve's insistence she said that she must bring her partner.

Duggie Holmes-Waterford decided, after consultation with his diary, that he could come, but refused for Alicia who, he said, had been rather upset by the murders.

'That leaves Bob,' Steve told Sonia. 'No use ringing him until the pubs close.'

'Do we have to have him?' asked Sonia, wrinkling her nose. 'He 's such a revolting little man.'

'He goes too far sometimes, I admit,' said Steve. 'But he has his good points and he can be funny when he's not completely sloshed. Anyway, this is an investigation; we can't pick and choose our guests, we've got to have the characters who were there when Vickers died.'

'Supposing they start asking awkward questions?' suggested Sonia. 'It could be very embarrassing; I suppose you hadn't thought of that?'

Steve's face hardened at the reminder that he dwelt in a glass house. 'We'll stick to opportunity and leave motive alone,' he said. 'Anyway, our affairs are probably common knowledge by now.'

Sonia was plainly annoyed. 'You don't care tuppence about my reputation, that's obvious,' she said.

On Saturday the frost loosened its grip. The countryside lost its tinselled look and took on homelier hues of brown and green. But it was still not fit to hunt; the ground was treacherous—greasy on the surface and bone hard below.

Browning, back from his expedition to see the Vickers

family, joined Flecker in London to help in the search for Mrs. Basset. Flecker had been encouraged by the Assistant Commissioner's attitude. It was a strange sensation, he thought, when your chief appeared to have more confidence in you than you had in yourself. But, as he hunted Bassets unsuccessfully through the London streets, he began to feel that his long shot had been too long, that the A.C.'s confidence was misplaced, and that Fox would have the last laugh.

On Saturday evening, Bob Bewley was the first of Steve's guests to arrive. Bewley wore such a conspiratorial air that Steve felt sure that Sonia would notice and realize the plan had been preconceived. But Bob was in one of his good moods; determined to please, he talked to Sonia while Steve finished organizing the drinks and, despite her avowed antagonism, she felt herself falling under his spell.

The Chadwicks came next. In defiance of fashion Commander Chadwick was always punctual. He took it that if people asked you for six, they meant six and he would arrive on the dot and expect to find his hostess dressed and ready to receive him. He had come to the Dentons armed with a writing-pad and pencil.

Steve thought that Hilary looked tired and that even Elizabeth was not her usual vivacious self. We're all in it, he thought; even the most innocent among us are affected. Bob's perfectly right; it's time we did something.

Antonia Brockenhurst had cleaned herself up for the occasion and wore a black skirt and a gay blouse, but Miss

Chiswick-Norton was still in slacks, with which she wore a man's shirt, a tie, and a riding jacket. Colonel Holmes-Waterford came attired as a country gentleman, in a brown suit and a buff waistcoat.

Steve said, 'Now that we're all here, who'd like to be chairman? What about you, Commander—you're senior to the rest of us.'

'No, no,' Charlie answered. 'That's your job, Steve; you called us together.'

Steve said, 'I'm the host; I'm dealing with the drinks.' And Sonia, suddenly reminded of her position, said, 'Do sit down, everyone; I hope there are enough chairs.'

They sat in a semi-circle facing the electric panel. It was unnecessary to cluster round it, because the flat possessed efficient central heating, but they were all used to a fire as the focal point of a room. Then Bob formally proposed that Charlie Chadwick should be chairman and Duggie Holmes-Waterford put it to the meeting. Everyone agreed.

'Very well, then,' said Chadwick, 'I'll do my best. But I'm not sure I'm in a very enviable position. I think that if we're not very careful we're all going to lose the rest of our friends, or such of our friends as are here.'

'Oh no, surely not. We must look on it as a purely scientific investigation,' said Duggie. 'Nothing personal allowed. Call us to order, Charlie. You're the man for that, we all know.'

'It's a great deal easier in the hunting field,' answered Charlie, with the slight relaxation of his face that served for a smile.

'I've never known a field master who could control his field with so little cursin' and swearin',' said Bob, 'and I've hunted with a good many packs. If looks could kill some of yours would, Charlie.'

'Murder by glance,' said Elizabeth with false brightness. 'Perhaps Charlie killed Guy with a look.'

'But not Clara,' Charlie answered. 'What are our terms of reference, Steve?'

'Opportunity,' answered the vet. 'Opportunity and method. Some of us have motives, but I doubt if it would do much good to discuss them.'

'Quite, and the police seemed to know all about the motives anyway,' said Duggie. 'I'm quite astounded by what they've found out in that line; we can't help them there. It's the actual poisoning of Vickers at the party that we may still be able to throw some light on.'

'I don't believe he *was* poisoned at the party,' said Elizabeth. I still believe that someone, one of the doctors probably, has made a ghastly mistake.'

'Nonsense,' said her husband, who had heard her express this view before. 'You've got to face facts, Elizabeth, and medical evidence of that nature counts as fact.'

'Well, it oughtn't to,' argued Elizabeth. 'Get hold of a few more doctors and I bet you could find a conflicting opinion. Have one little boy with you and you'll be told the name of every aeroplane that flies over, have two little boys and there'll be an argument over each one.'

'How very right you are, Elizabeth,' exclaimed Duggie. 'Even though, in this case, I can't entirely agree with you,

176

I am prepared to admit a margin of error.'

'Order, order,' said Charlie. 'The chairman's wife is not to be encouraged. Our terms of reference do *not*, repeat *not*, permit discussion of the medical evidence.'

'I'm interested in the method,' said Steve. 'The Chief Inspector seemed to think that we should have noticed someone fishing for a piece of cork or a dead fly in his drink.'

'I resent that suggestion, I utterly refute it,' exclaimed Charlie with assumed anger. 'None of my guests would have dared to imply such a thing.'

'Take the Chief Inspector up for slander,' suggested Hilary.

'Yes, actually he asked me that one too,' said Antonia. 'As far as I could make out he seemed to think the murderer would mix the poison in his own drink and, if he was seen, would pretend he was fishing for a piece of cork.'

'And then he would swap the drinks,' said Steve. 'Which would make it more difficult for the people who weren't drinking cocktails.'

'Namely Mark, Antonia and Elizabeth,' Charlie told him.

'I think the Big Noise suspects Mark of having whipped up Clara's drink and poisoned that,' said Bob. 'He's been taking an outsize interest in it, or rather in the fact that she finished up the evening without a glass.'

'Did she indeed?' asked Charlie. 'I knew the Chief Inspector was trying to find someone who had, but I'd no idea he'd done it. Perhaps he is getting somewhere then, in his own quiet way.'

'*Could* Mark have taken Clara's drink, poisoned it, and passed it on to Vickers?' asked Steve.

'No, of course he couldn't,' Hilary spoke with certainty. 'He hadn't nearly enough time. He only left the door end of the room when he went to find Clara. He would hardly have had time to pour poison into Guy's glass, much less find Clara, get her glass and all the rest of it. You were talking to Guy during the time when Mark is supposed to have poisoned him,' she went on, turning to Duggie. 'Did you see anything?'

'No. But in this company I'm bound to admit I wouldn't have seen anything,' Duggie answered her. 'You see, I wasn't looking towards the chimneypiece, I had my back to the fire.'

'Guy's glass wasn't on the chimneypiece,' said Hilary. 'It was in his hand.'

'If that was so it would have been more or less impossible to poison him,' said Steve. 'You've got to look at it like this, Hilary,' he went on. 'Vickers was poisoned, in front of us all. That's the evidence, and, as your father says, we've got to accept it. If Vickers held his glass in his hand all evening, he couldn't have been poisoned without his consent. By that I mean it's just possible that someone said, "try one of these tablets, old man, they prevent hangovers"; or something equally unlikely. But, if that had happened, I'm perfectly certain he would have told us when he was dying. I asked him several questions about what he'd had to eat and drink, but he insisted that he'd taken no drugs, no medicines and eaten only his ordinary meals. And that was before they filled him up with dope; his mind was crystal clear. He *must* have put his glass down at sometime in the evening, and at that moment it was either poisoned or switched.'

'He didn't put it down while I was talking to him,' said Hilary, unshaken by Steve's arguments.

'How many of us talked to him?' asked Bob. 'Hilary and Duggie have confessed that they did. I didn't actually speak to him, but I suppose I could have switched the glasses when I collected Clara. Clara had plenty of opportunity, of course; anyone else?'

'I didn't speak to him until he felt sick,' said Steve.

'I talked to him for a few minutes at the beginning of the party,' said Elizabeth. 'But the conversation was general; I don't think I could have slipped anything into his glass.'

'I hope I'm not speaking out of turn,' said Miss Chiswick-Norton, smiling toothily round the half-circle of faces in an attempt to ingratiate herself. 'I mean, I know I wasn't there or anything—on Friday night, I mean—and probably you'll think I'm silly; but it seems to me that Commander Chadwick could have done it as easy as pie. Poisoned poor Mr. Vickers, I mean. He'd only got to take the shaker thing out to the kitchen and put one poisoned cocktail in it; give that to poor Mr. Vickers, go out again, wash the shaker thing, fill it up with an unpoisoned cocktail and come back. No one would have been any the wiser, if you see what I mean.'

'Quite, quite,' said Steve. 'But the Commander hasn't a motive.'

'We're not concerned with motives,' Charlie told him. 'You're perfectly right, Miss Chiswick-Norton. I had by far the biggest opportunity. Actually Scotland Yard is well aware of that and I suspect my past has been probed fairly thoroughly. However, I am more than willing to head the list of suspects.'

'And after you,' said Miss Chiswick-Norton, her smile turning wolfish, 'must come your daughter.'

'I don't see why,' protested Elizabeth promptly.

'I do,' Hilary answered. 'I talked to Guy much more than anyone else.'

'That's right, you see what I mean. You had plenty of time. You could have slipped the poison in when it was convenient; you wouldn't have had to rush it like anyone else. You don't mind my speaking frankly, do you? I mean that's why we're here, isn't it? To find out all we can and you could have done it easily. *Easily*,' she repeated, and there was something unpleasantly insinuating about her tone.

'But I didn't,' said Hilary calmly.

'No, of course you didn't,' Duggie Holmes-Waterford backed her up. 'No one in their senses would dream of suggesting such a thing. *You* could have had no possible reason to poison Guy.'

'However,' said Charlie, 'she did have the opportunity. We'll put her second on the list. Now we want a candidate for third place. What about my wife?' he asked, a little sarcastically.

'No, she's a hundred to one outsider,' objected Bob. 'Who else talked to Vickers?'

'I did,' answered Duggie; 'and, of course, Clara.'

'Clara could have bumped him off,' said Bob. 'But why? We can discuss her motive, Mr. Chairman, since she is beyond embarrassment or denial.'

'Why indeed?' asked Duggie.

'I have a feeling that our policeman thinks Mark might have put her up to it,' said Bob. 'I don't think it's frightfully likely, myself.'

'It's an idiotic idea,' said Elizabeth firmly.

'Well, we'd better put Clara third and Duggie fourth on the list,' said Charlie. 'Now, what about the rest of you? If I were the murderer, I would have taken jolly good care not to be seen near my victim, so I'm more suspicious of those who haven't admitted talking to Guy than I am of those who have. Which of you went anywhere near the fireplace?'

'Me,' answered Bob. 'I went to collect Clara from Vickers. I keep pointing out that I could have popped the lethal dose in then.'

'Mr. Broughton,' said Antonia. 'He went quite near, but I must say I never saw him put anything in.'

'You were watching him closely?' asked Duggie.

'Not all that closely,' answered Antonia. 'It was just that Colonel Clinkerton had told me about having a joint master and I wondered whether Mr. Broughton was going to say anything about it to Guy Vickers. But he didn't.'

'That's interesting,' said Charlie. 'It sounds to me as though you would have seen if Mark had attempted any funny stuff.'

'Yes, but I wouldn't like to swear to anything,' Antonia

181

told him. 'I don't feel certain about it, you see; not one way or the other.'

'It looks as though Mr. Broughton did do it through his wife; the murder, I mean,' said Miss Chiswick-Norton. 'She would have been too gaga to know what she was doing, poor thing. I mean if she had known, it would have been obvious what his next step was—to kill her, I mean—and she would have had the sense not to start the ball rolling.'

'You are suggesting that Mark told Clara that she was to poison Vickers because he was trying to gain control of the hounds, I take it?' asked Duggie.

'Yes, I mean that's what he would have told her but, of course, we know that there was quite a different reason,' said Norty, with a malicious glance at Hilary.

Charlie Chadwick said, 'No motives, please,' in an apparently unmoved voice. But the air was heavy with embarrassment and Hilary's face set in stony lines.

Suddenly Sonia, who had hitherto taken no part in the discussion, came to life.

'Oh!' One hand fluttered to her throat as she gave a little cry of horror. 'Did someone say that *Clara* gave Guy the poison? Because she offered *me* a cocktail. She mumbled something about not wanting it. She said that she hadn't *licked* it. Oh, Steve, supposing I'd taken it? Then *I* should have died. But I thought, I don't want anything you've touched; I wouldn't fancy it, I might catch something.'

'You're sure about that, Sonia?' asked Steve. 'It might be very important, so you want to be quite certain of your facts.'

'Yes, I've told you, haven't I?' Sonia sounded a little hysterical as the idea of her nearness to death sank in.

Charlie asked, 'Does this put a new complexion on things, or are we still more or less where we were before?'

'Well, I suppose Clara *could* have gone right off her rocker,' said Bob, 'and just rushed round with an urge to poison someone. Alternatively, if Mark had put her up to poisoning Vickers she could have got a bit mixed up and offered it to Sonia first.'

'It all sounds a lot too far fetched to me,' said Charlie. 'I don't think Clara was "off her rocker" as Bob puts it, and I'm sure Mark wouldn't have used her as a stooge.'

'I entirely agree with you, Charlie,' said Duggie warmly. 'It sounds quite unlike Mark. I don't want to seem crushing, but I doubt whether Mrs. Denton's experience throws any new light on the matter. Have you told the police about it?' he asked Sonia.

'No, I'd quite forgotten about it until now.'

'We'd better tell Flecker,' said Charlie. 'Then it's up to him. Will you tell him, Steve? Or shall I?'

'You'd better give him a report on the lot, and then he can follow it up or not, as he likes.'

'You'll have to wait until Monday,' Bob broke in. 'Mrs. Gordon tells me they've gone back to London.'

Steve said, 'Well, we've discovered one or two things and if you agree, Mr. Chairman, and if everybody has exhausted their ideas on this matter, I suggest we have another drink and talk about something else.'

'I can't think about anything else,' objected Sonia. 'You

183

don't seem to realize, Steve; I mightn't be here. I might be dead. You might have all gone to my funeral yesterday, instead of to Clara's.'

'If you ask me,' said Antonia, 'the police are barking up quite a different tree. They've been all round Langley asking for a Mrs. Basset who lived there years ago. I wondered if they'd stopped suspecting us when I heard about it.'

'Perhaps Guy *did* have something to eat or drink before he came to the party then,' said Elizabeth, her face brightening. 'Wouldn't it be wonderful if in the end, it turned out to be nothing to do with any of us?'

'Don't forget there's still Clara's death to be accounted for,' said Charlie.

But Elizabeth was not to be downcast. 'Oh, I'd forgive the police anything,' she said, 'if they'd come round in the morning and tell us that this nightmare was over; that they'd caught the murderer, a man we'd never heard of, just a murderer; the sort one rather enjoys reading about in the Sunday papers.'

'But even the Sunday paper murderers aren't born to it,' said Hilary. 'They must have families and friends too. But still,' she added, 'the police do seem a bit less suspicious of Mark; apparently there hasn't been a copper outside the house all day.'

CHAPTER EIGHTEEN

BOB BEWLEY WAS WRONG. Flecker and Browning were back in Lollington on Saturday night. Having traced the elusive Mrs. Basset to Manchester, they had handed over the search to the C.I.D. of that city and returned to Wintshire.

Charlie Chadwick telephoned the Dog and Duck on Sunday morning, intending to leave a message asking Flecker to come over to Hazebrook on his return; but, hearing that 'he was just next door in the saloon bar,' he asked Mrs. Gordon to fetch him.

Chadwick disapproved of the long gossipy telephone conversations in which his wife and daughter loved to indulge and believed in cutting the conventional niceties to nothing. Now, to Flecker, he said, 'I want a word with you, Chief Inspector. Can you come round?'

'Yes, of course,' answered Flecker. 'Shall I come right away?'

'Yes,' said Charlie, replacing the receiver.

Flecker called to Browning, 'They want us over at Hazebrook.'

'What for?' inquired Browning, joining him in the hall.

'I've no idea,' Flecker answered. 'Old Chadwick must have served in the days when signals were sent by flags, and he didn't want to hoist too many this morning. Just said he'd like a word with me.'

'Well, he's not one to get carried away by nothing,' said Browning. 'I'll nip out and get the car.'

Elizabeth Chadwick let the detectives in. 'This shows great devotion to duty,' she said. 'My husband didn't expect to find you at Lollington; don't the police ever have days off?'

'The Chief Inspector's a terrible slave-driver, madam,' said Browning with a smile.

As they left their coats in the hall, Charlie Chadwick appeared at the drawing-room door.

'Good morning,' he said. 'You didn't take long to get here. I'm not sure that my information is worthy of such dispatch.'

'Any information is gratefully received,' Flecker told him.

'Isn't it wonderful to be warm again?' said Elizabeth. 'Or comparatively warm, anyway. I do hate the winter.'

'We'll have another freeze up in February, bound to,' said Browning. 'It's no good you expecting the spring yet.'

Flecker looked at Chadwick, 'Well, Commander?'

'Last night,' said Charlie carefully, 'we were invited to drinks with the Dentons. It was agreed among us that we should discuss the murders, objectively, with a view to pooling our common experiences and helping the police. I was made chairman of the discussion and have been asked to report to you.'

'Oh dear,' said Flecker. 'Carry on, sir.'

'Nothing very startling transpired. The general idea seemed to be that Mrs. Broughton murdered Vickers either because she was mad or because her husband told her to. We were working those lines when Mrs. Denton remembered that Mrs. Broughton had offered her a

186

cocktail during the party.'

'Oh, she did, did she,' said Flecker, without any sign of excitement.

The Chadwicks were disappointed. 'Bob said you were very interested in Clara's missing glass, that's why we thought this might be important,' Elizabeth explained. 'But we heard you were looking for a Mrs. Basset now.'

'Another salient fact which emerged,' said Commander Chadwick, referring to some notes, 'was that Antonia Brockenhurst was actually watching Mark when he passed by Vickers and she didn't see him put anything in his glass.'

'The Chief Inspector's not interested in Mark any more,' Elizabeth told her husband. 'You know Hilary said there isn't a policeman on guard or anything now.'

Flecker tugged distractedly at his forelock. 'Don't tell me you discussed all this at the Dentons'?' he said.

'Yes,' Charlie answered. 'We found we knew quite a bit between us; we—'

'Who was there?' Flecker interrupted him.

'The Dentons, three of us, Captain Bewley and Colonel Holmes-Waterford; oh, and Miss Brockenhurst brought her partner, that awful redheaded Chiswick-Norton woman,' answered Elizabeth.

Flecker was on his feet before she had finished.

'Sorry,' he said. 'I think we'd better go.' And Browning, recognizing the almost imperceptible signs of great urgency, shot by his chief, collected their overcoats and dashed down the garden path to the car.

'Where to?' he asked, as Flecker slipped in beside him.

'The kennels.'

The Chadwicks, rather startled by the abrupt departure of the detectives, stood on their front doorstep and heard the car roar away up the road.

'What on earth was that in aid of?' asked Elizabeth.

'Can't imagine,' answered Charlie. 'Perhaps they've been going to American films.'

They were tearing down the high road before Browning ventured a question. 'What's up now, sir?' he asked.

'I don't know,' said Flecker. 'With any luck, nothing. But I'll feel happier when I've made sure that Broughton is still at home. The *idiocy* of those people; don't they realize that by the time you've done two murders you don't think twice before committing your third?'

Browning accelerated. Sounding the horn almost continuously, he drove down the twisting road to Little Lapworth at a highly unsuitable speed. 'Lucky it's Sunday,' he remarked, as he negotiated a corner entirely on the wrong side of the road. Flecker said nothing but sighed with relief as they turned from the road into the lane which led to the kennels. He was out of the car and doubling towards the front door before Browning had pulled up at the gate. Browning turned the car and then followed him into the house.

The children had gone to church. Nan couldn't say where Mr. Broughton was; he'd gone out in the car, with all the dogs, about ten minutes ago. So much Flecker had elicited before Browning joined him. Had Mr. Broughton had a letter? he asked. Had he telephoned anyone? Had anyone telephoned him?

'Letters on a Sunday?' said Nan, 'Never.' But she thought she had heard some talk of a note.

'We'll try the office,' said Flecker.

There on the desk, spread out flat in the middle of the blotter and weighted by a pencil at either end, lay the note. Without touching it, Flecker and Browning read:

'If you would like information re the death of your wife meet me at Crossways barn at 11 a.m. Sunday. Come alone or I shall not appear.'

'He meant us to see it,' said Flecker. He hurried to the door and called loudly, 'Can you tell me where Crossways barn is, Miss Hatch?'

'I don't know, I'm sure,' said Nan. 'You'd better ask Codding or Mr. Philips out in the stable.'

'Never mind.' Flecker swung round and pointed to the large-scale map pinned to the wall of the office. 'Here,' he said to Browning, 'this is the West Wintshire Hunt country. Come and give me a hand; it's bound to be here somewhere.'

Browning picked up something from the desk. 'This note's in his own handwriting; it's a bit disguised, but look.' He held up Mark's engagement diary for Flecker to see.

'Never mind about that,' answered Flecker sharply. 'Come and look for Crossways barn; you take the right half.'

'Supposing it's a blind?' protested Browning as he looked. 'Ten to one he's nipped off in the opposite direction.'

'Here it is; up above Rollhurst Farm. Come on, we'll take this with us.' Flecker tore the map from the wall and looked at his watch. Five minutes to eleven.' He was in the hall before he had finished speaking.

'Turn left at the top of the lane and then it's the first on your right,' he said as Browning started the car. Rollhurst was higher than Lapworth and more remote. The road which led to it was very narrow and climbed steeply with many sharp turns. At last they reached the top of the hill, emerging suddenly through the belt of trees.

'Straight through the village,' ordered Flecker. A few scattered cottages comprised the village and then they were out in the open. On both sides of the tiny road stretched arable land, an unfenced patchwork of stubble and plough that crowned the whole of the windswept hilltop.

'Any moment now there should be a right turn,' said Flecker. 'There it is.'

'Poor ruddy tyres,' said Browning as they screamed round into the lane.

'That must be Keeper's Cottage. In a minute we'll see the barn ahead—if we're right.'

The lane continued stony as far as the hollow which sheltered Keeper's Cottage but beyond that it became a cart track and where it rose to join the fields again the car baulked, its wheels spinning ineffectively as they tried to climb the slope.

'Leave her,' said Flecker, jumping out. He glanced at his watch and began to run. It was seven minutes past eleven.

Once he was out of the hollow he could see the barn standing in the open at the junction of four grassy cart tracks which met among the plough. Beyond was a wood; he wished that he had known the way through the wood. Browning caught up with him. 'Lucky it looks the other way,' said Flecker. 'Will you take the left side?' Browning, who was no stayer, could only nod.

As they reached the barn they both slowed to a walk and Flecker's heart lifted with relief as he heard the sound of angry voices from within. Browning appeared round the front of the barn at the same moment as Flecker, and, from opposite sides of the great door, they peered in. Mark Broughton, revolver in hand, stood in a threatening attitude. Cringing back against the bales of straw was Colonel Douglas Holmes-Waterford.

'Good morning ,' said Flecker.

Both men jumped round in surprise. Holmes-Waterford spoke first:

'My God, I'm glad to see you, Chief Inspector,' he said. 'Broughton seems to have gone raving mad.' He laughed shakily. 'I thought my last moment had come.'

Mark just stood and stared, an expression of disbelief on his stunned face.

'I'll have that gun, please sir,' said Browning, and took it from his unresisting hand.

Flecker turned to Duggie. 'Colonel Holmes-Waterford,' he said in an official voice, 'I would like you to accompany me to the police station. I have some questions to ask you about the murder of Mrs. Broughton and this incident.'

'Don't be a B.F., Chief Inspector. Mark's your man,' answered Duggie.

'I don't think so,' said Flecker. 'But anyway you can still make a statement. Where's your car, Mr. Broughton? Ours has stuck in the mud.'

'On the far side of the copse,' Mark answered.

'Then perhaps you'll take us down to Melborough? We'll come back for ours later.'

'Anything you like,' said Mark vaguely. 'But I'm afraid it's full of dogs.' Then he asked, 'Did you know that the Colonel here intended shooting me? He dam' near did too; I only just saw him in time.'

'We had our suspicions,' said Flecker. 'How did you get the gun away from him?'

'We had a bit of a scrap,' Mark answered and, reminded that he had been rolling on the barn floor, began to pull the straws out of his hair and brush them from his clothes.

'That's your story,' said Duggie. 'But you can't get away from the fact that it's your revolver. He telephoned me last night, Chief Inspector, and asked me to meet him here. You must have seen for yourself that he was just about to shoot me when you came in.'

'I think,' said Flecker, 'that, if you have no objection, we'd better make sure there are no more guns concealed on your persons.'

'No objection whatsoever,' answered Duggie. 'In fact I shall feel happier when I know that *all* our friend's teeth are drawn.'

Flecker ran his hands over Duggie's pockets, while Browning did the same to Mark. There were no ominous bulges, but Flecker had felt an envelope in the pocket of Duggie's hacking jacket, and, satisfied that there were no more guns, whipped it out.

'Give that back at once,' commanded Duggie. 'I gave you permission to search me for offensive weapons, not to take possession of my private correspondence.'

'As it is addressed "To whom it may concern" and appears to be written in Mr. Broughton's handwriting, I hardly think it can be described as your private correspondence,' Flecker answered as he opened the envelope. 'I, Mark Broughton,' he began and then finished reading in silence. 'It's your confession,' he told Mark, 'to the murders of Vickers and your wife.'

'Look out!' shouted Browning, as Duggie made a dash for the door. Flecker stuffed the confession in his pocket and joined in the pursuit. Browning had already drawn level with his quarry, who wheeled round and took to the plough land to avoid him. Flecker closed in; he had not played rugger for the police for nothing, and, tackling low, he deposited Duggie face downwards among the furrows. Browning produced his handcuffs. 'We don't want to take any more chances, sir, do we?' he asked.

'No,' Flecker agreed. And Browning handcuffed himself to Duggie, before helping Flecker yank him to his feet.

Flecker said, 'Colonel Holmes-Waterford, I am arresting you for the attempted murder of Mr. Broughton. You are not obliged to say anything in answer to this charge, but whatever you say will be taken down in writing and may be used in evidence.'

Duggie didn't answer, he had not yet regained his

breath. His face and clothes were now covered in mud as well as in straw and he looked quite unlike his usual immaculate self. They led him back to the barn.

Mark read through the confession with slow concentration. 'This is diabolical, Duggie,' he said. 'Now I understand why you were trying to shoot me in the face from a range of two feet. He was lying on those straw bales,' he went on, turning to Flecker, 'and he'd fixed up the door so that it would only open a couple of feet. He'd have got me right in the face, only my coat caught on the latch and I stopped and turned away to pull it free; that spoiled his calculations. He moved and I saw the gun and ducked as he fired. If he'd got me you would have taken it as suicide—my revolver, a note in my writing.'

'That's your story,' said Duggie, producing a handkerchief and attempting to wipe the mud from his face with his free hand. 'And anyone with a grain of intelligence could tell that it was merely the fabrication of a mentally disturbed mind. If the Chief Inspector chooses to believe you, let him, but my God, I shall get my own back if he does. I shall raise Cain. I've got friends in high places, Chief Inspector. I shall sue and it won't just be for wrongful arrest. I shall extract retribution for this indignity; retribution in full and with interest.'

'Well, let's get down to the police station, then you can make a statement,' said Flecker equably. 'I'll have that document back, please, Mr. Broughton.'

'That document's another of his fiendish tricks,' Duggie spoke with acrimony. 'Obviously he planted it in my pocket while we were scrapping. He meant to shoot himself if he found the game was up. Can't you see it, Chief Inspector? He was prepared for every eventuality. My God, it's a nice situation. And I thought he was my best friend! It would be a bitter pill to swallow if it wasn't all too obvious that the poor fellow's raving mad.'

'Come along now, Colonel,' said Browning, as Flecker led the way out of the barn. 'I don't know about anyone else, but I could do with a nice cup of tea.'

CHAPTER NINETEEN

IT TOOK Flecker and Browning a couple of days to tie up the loose ends of the case. Then, on Tuesday evening, they drove to Lapworth for the last time. They had promised to have an off-duty drink with Mark, before returning to London.

The detectives were rather surprised by the warmth with which they were welcomed, both by the Broughtons and by the Chadwicks, who had also come in to drinks. Mark produced champagne. 'We're not celebrating,' he said; 'it's just that we can't face gin.'

It was Elizabeth who brought the conversation round to the murders and when she did so Mark, ignoring their arguments and indignation, sent the children to feed the dogs.

'Now,' said Elizabeth, drawing closer to the fire, 'I've got several questions to ask you, Chief Inspector. You don't mind, do you? Charlie says that it's contrary to the ethics of your profession to tell the laymen anything, but we're hardly laymen, are we? We're sort of amateurs now; we've been so heavily involved.'

Flecker grinned. 'Let's have the questions,' he said, 'before I say whether I'll answer them or not.'

Elizabeth thought for a moment before she spoke. 'What I really want to know,' she said, 'is how you knew that it was Duggie. I hadn't the least idea and though now, people are beginning to say that he always had peculiar eyes or gave them the creeps, I'm sure it had never previously entered their heads he might be the murderer.'

Flecker pushed back his hair. 'Well,' he said, 'it wasn't very difficult because there were so few real suspects. But, I admit that the Colonel didn't seem a very likely murderer of Vickers. That was what put Hollis off. In fact, I never could see how Vickers was murdered. You all told me that it couldn't have been done at the party, and really, sometimes I felt like believing you. It seemed likely that Mrs. Broughton was involved in some way. And when Mrs. Chadwick told me she'd heard her told not to have more than one drink, I began to make wild guesses about what might have happened to the second drink. The right one evaded me for some time. There were various other oddities; there was Mrs. Broughton's extra and unexplained supply of gin; there was the Colonel's insistence that he was Mr. Broughton's oldest friend and his strange habit of dropping damning hints. His comment on the childless state of his "oldest friend" was an error. I didn't notice it at the time, but later when Anstruther, our pathologist, told us that Mrs. Broughton had borne a child, I realized that the Colonel's choice of words implied that he knew she *could* bear one. I also remembered that Mrs. Broughton had only really despaired after her failure to rescue the small child from the river at Langley. That reduced my suspects to four; I knew that if I was on the right track, the murderer was a man other than Mr. Broughton who had been present at the cocktail party.

'I had made my choice, but I must admit that I was hardly in a position to make an arrest, when Mr. Broughton precipitated me into it. However, now that our

197

colleagues in Manchester have got Mrs. Basset, the foster-mother of the child, talking, everything has become a great deal clearer. Mrs. Basset knew that Mrs. Broughton was the mother, but she never learned the name of the father. She said that Mrs. Broughton was attached to the child in a rather unbalanced way and that she had insisted on the child being brought to Langley for a holiday, so that she would be able to see more of her without the risk of raising suspicion by constant visits to London. Mrs. Basset understood that the father lived locally and that he strongly disapproved of this holiday. Then, on the day of the child's death, Mrs. Broughton told Mrs. Basset that she had persuaded the father to come over and see his daughter in the hope that he would agree to some sort of arrangement; an adoption, Mrs. Basset thought. But apparently the child bore a likeness to her father and, though there seemed to be little doubt that if Mr. Broughton were told he would agree to adopt, there were difficulties confronting the father. A wife who must be deceived at all costs and, at the bottom of it all, money—that was what Mrs. Basset understood.'

Elizabeth said, 'Yes, I can see that. Alicia isn't a forgiving sort at all, and, of course, she did keep Duggie in great comfort.'

'Mrs. Basset never knew exactly what happened on the day of the child's death,' Flecker went on. 'Mrs. Broughton was so distraught afterwards that she never managed to get a coherent account. Apparently Mrs. Broughton took the child to a comparatively quiet spot along the riverbank and there met the father. He refused to agree to any of her plans, he said that the child was to be taken back to London and brought up there and a violent argument ensued. While they were arguing they forgot the child and she fell into the river. Mrs. Broughton went straight in after her, but she wasn't, I gather, much of a swimmer; the father, determined not to be involved at any cost, hurried away. According to Mrs. Basset, his defence was that he thought Mrs. Broughton had got hold of the child and would be all right, but Mrs. Broughton never really believed him and never forgave him. Mrs. Basset received a substantial sum to perjure herself at the inquest and we have been able to trace that payment and a monthly sum paid for the child's upkeep. It was actually paid to Mrs. Basset in cash, through a third party, but we have managed to identify the third party and he has admitted that he received the money by cheque from the Colonel.

'After the death of the child, Mrs. Broughton seems to have exercised a sort of despairing blackmail over the Colonel. Only a drunken oblivion was bearable and as this was his doing, he must supply the gin. We don't know, of course, exactly what passed between them, but we do know that far more gin was delivered to Lapworth Manor than was ever consumed there, that the Colonel was always in trouble with his wife for overspending his pension and the personal allowance she made him, and that, recently, the trouble between them had been coming to a head.'

'Where *did* he keep the poison?' asked Elizabeth. 'I'm sure that if Charlie was hiding jars of arsenic all over the

199

place I'd find them.'

'He brewed it in the wine cellar,' Flecker answered. 'He'd set himself up as a great authority on wines; no one was allowed to touch any of the cases that were delivered or to enter the cellar on any pretext; they didn't even know where he kept the keys. That had been necessary for the concealment of the gin supply, and it came in very handy when he decided that murder offered a way out of his difficulties. He brewed a fairly strong arsenical solution by soaking a certain brand of flypapers—those old-fashioned sticky ones that hang from the ceiling. Luckily for us he left a supply in the cellar, I suppose he was keeping it for future use; with it was the writing pad he'd used to write to Mr. Broughton and also a small bottle with traces of the solution still in it. You remember, Mr. Broughton, how in your confession he makes you describe the way in which you poisoned Vickers? Well, I imagine that that was precisely the method he used in his first attempt on Mrs. Broughton. "I eased the cork from the little bottle while it was still in my pocket. I took it out still concealed in my handkerchief and turned away as though to sneeze. I poured the arsenic into the half empty glass, which I had previously taken from my wife." It would have been easier than that for him, he would simply have drunk half his own cocktail, poisoned the remainder when no one was looking, and then changed glasses with Mrs. Broughton. Mrs. Denton seems to have been the only person who saw the deed. She thought she saw Mrs. Broughton upsetting her drink over the Colonel, but I've no doubt that it was the Colonel who engineered

200

the collision and that the steadying hand and the mopping up operation, which Mrs. Denton now remembers, masked the changeover of glasses. However, Mrs. Broughton had been told not to have more than one drink and she decided to give the lethal one away. As we know now, she actually offered it to Mrs. Denton before giving it to Vickers.

'Though, in a way, Vickers' death confused the issue so much that it was in the Colonel's favour, at the time of the murder he must have had to resort to some quick thinking. For, if Mrs. Broughton had sobered up, she might have realized what had happened and told Mr. Broughton or the police. He acted that same night. He told his wife at dinner that he had to see the secretary of the local Conservative Association, and he did visit him, but only for a few minutes of the hour and a quarter during which he was out. The rest of the time was spent in delivering a bottle of poisoned gin to the Broughtons' summerhouse.'

'You mean he knew that Guy had been given the poisoned drink?' asked Hilary. 'And that he just stood there and watched him drink it?'

'I'm afraid so,' answered Flecker.

Hilary shuddered.

'The summerhouse,' Flecker went on, 'was, of course, the dumping ground for the weekly gin ration and I suppose the Colonel was afraid of fingerprints, a lost button or some other incriminating evidence and so he burned it down. And then there was the revolver; Miss Hatch was able to clear that up for us. Apparently Mrs. Broughton had taken it to the summerhouse one day soon after the death of the child, with the intention of committing suicide, but she told Nan that the Colonel had happened to look in and caught her at it and he had taken the revolver away. How he must have cursed himself for that act afterwards.

'Of course, like most murderers, the Colonel expected to get away with the murder of Mrs. Broughton, and I think that, actually, he had more chance than most. Dr. Skindle knew all about Mrs. Broughton and if she had died, without the poisoning of Vickers to draw his attention to the symptoms of arsenical poisoning, he would probably have signed her death certificate without a murmur, for there was no doubt, that she was drinking herself to death. The trouble with the Colonel was that he couldn't wait; she was an ever-increasing risk to his marriage and so he embarked on what he thought would be a hurrying-up operation and nearly committed three murders in the process.'

For a few moments no one spoke. Then Mark broke the silence.

'That business in the barn gave me the nastiest moment of my life,' he said. 'Not when he let the thing off at me, but when you walked in and caught me pointing it at Duggie—my own revolver. And Duggie coolly saying, "Thank God you've come, Chief Inspector; Broughton seems to have gone raving mad." I've never been so frightened in my life; I thought you were going to believe him.'

'It served you right,' said Flecker, 'for playing Cops and

Robbers with him. No one in their senses would rush off to meet a murderer unarmed and alone. But I'm afraid the Colonel knew you too well; he knew just what sort of bait you would rise to.'

'I thought I behaved rather intelligently,' protested Mark. 'After all, I did leave the note for you.'

'That wouldn't have been much use if Commander Chadwick hadn't told us about the Dentons' party,' answered Flecker.

'You simply shot out of the house,' said Elizabeth. 'I thought that Miss Chiswick-Norton must be murdering Antonia Brockenhurst; I don't quite know why.'

Browning laughed. 'The Chief Inspector gave Miss Chiswick-what's it a talking to,' he said. 'I've never heard you speak like it before, sir. Tore strips off her, he did, yesterday afternoon.'

'Why, what had she done?' asked Elizabeth.

'Now that is an unethical question,' said Flecker. 'Or rather it would be unethical for me to answer it. Let's say that a raspberry was deserved and duly delivered, and leave it at that.'

'Well I think you're terribly clever,' said Elizabeth, 'I should never even have guessed about the Colonel. I should have been like Hollis and gone for Mark if I hadn't known that he was much too nice to be a murderer.'

'Oh, there's nothing clever about it,' answered Flecker. 'Detection's rather like being dumped in the middle of a maze and told to find your way out. You choose a path and start walking; if you're lucky it turns out to be the right path, and if you're not, you just go back to the

203

middle and start again. Like most things in life, it's a matter of perseverance really.'

'I think I would describe that as an over-simplification,' said Charlie, with a faint relaxation of his mouth.

'We must go.' Flecker put down his glass and got to his feet. 'Or we shall have Mrs. Browning after us.'

Mark said, 'Well, Chief Inspector, it was nice of you to come, both tonight and professionally.'

'And to satisfy my wife's curiosity,' said Charlie.

As they put on their coats in the hall, they could hear the voices of Deb and Jon singing lustily. The words of the song, which seemed to be a topical version of 'Daisy', came to them clearly:

> *'They'll tie you up with wire*
> *In the back of a black maria,*
> *So ring your bell*
> *And pedal like hell,*
> *On a bicycle made for two.'*

'There doesn't seem to be much wrong with them,' said Browning.

Mark saw the detectives off and then, as the sound of their car faded, he turned back towards the house. Elizabeth came tearing down the garden path.

'Quick, Mark,' she said, 'the Chief Inspector's gloves.'

'It's too late,' Mark told her. 'He's gone. Never mind, we'll put them in a glass case and hang them up beside the foxes' masks in the office.'